ADVANCE PRAISE FOR JA
AND THE GHOST OF ZUMBI

"Suzanne Litrel IS Jackie Tempo. Litrel's adolescent travel experiences backed by a vast world history teaching background, produces a valuable and exciting motivation for young readers to think about history. Story telling and historical fiction blend in *Jackie Tempo and the Ghost of Zumbi* to do just that---excite young readers to enjoy history."

John Maunu
World History teacher
Grosse Ile High School, Michigan
College Board World History consultant
Advance Placement World History Reader/Table Leader
2002-2003 Michigan Education Association Global and Diversity Educator of the Year

****

"*Jackie Tempo and the Ghost of Zumbi* is a fast-paced and fun-filled adventure that both entertains and educates. Once again, our 20th century heroine, 15 year old Jackie Tempo, is magically transported through time to 18th century Brazil, where she comes face to face with a Brazilian medicine woman with strange powers and a 20th century villain. Combining elements of mystery, suspense, and a bit of teenage romance, the author interweaves a poignant coming of age story with vivid descriptions of a time and place where trading in human cargo was the norm. Set against a backdrop of a significant world historical event, the author deftly explores the impact of the Atlantic slave trade through the eyes of a teen who experiences firsthand the horrors of slavery. As the story unfolds and Jackie forms relationships with those in another time and place, she begins to appreciate the complexity of the people and cultures she encounters. And, just as Jackie develops in her analysis of historical events and the people affected by those events, the reader also gains a more personal understanding of history than that usually provided by textbooks. Tidbits of historical information, integral to understanding both the characters and the context of the time, are seamlessly incorporated throughout the storyline. Rich in detail with engaging characters, multiple story lines, and a plot with more than enough twists to keep the reader in suspense, I highly recommend *Jackie Tempo and the Ghost of Zumbi* for teens, parents, and teachers alike."

Linda Black, Ph.d
Secondary Education Department
Stephen F. Austin State University

AP World History Exam Reader, Table Leader, and Question Leader
Note: Dr. Black was on the original AP World History Test Design Committee

***

"Jackie Tempo and the Ghost of Zumbi, the second in the Jackie Tempo series, is infused with the attitudes and techniques of world history, bringing to young readers an exciting story that effortlessly informs as well as delights. While Jackie Tempo's mother grew up "among rare volumes—dusty portals to other worlds," a metaphor that reminds young readers of the power of fiction, Jackie is quite literally dragged by her mysterious book through a space-time portal into other worlds (Ming China in the first book in the series and 17th century Brazil in the current book).

"The Ghost of Zumbi weaves many strands into an exciting young adult offering:

- a teenager who doesn't fit into her new school
- a budding friendship/romance with the popular, older boy who has been hired as her tutor, an adventure ranging from a modern New England town to a maroon settlement the Brazilian forests during the 17th century
- an active, energetic heroine who rescues other people instead of waiting to be rescued by the handsome prince
- a magical book from Samarkand that can transport its owner across space and time,
- a conflict between good and evil as Jackie attempts to rescue her parents and to prevent a rift in space/time
- a history lesson on the quilombo settlements (communities of maroons or escaped slaves) in Brazil and the horrors of plantation slavery
- a friendship between wise women across times and cultures,
- a peek into an exciting world history classroom (perhaps modeled on the author's?), and
- a subtle exposure to multiple perspectives of world cultures through the use of proverbs from Brazil and Africa.

The Ghost of Zumbi—and the basic premise of the Jackie Tempo series—allow young readers to travel through world history with a sympathetic, daring character of their own age. These stories are a boon to teachers of world history, helping them get students imaginatively engaged in the essential themes and processes of the discipline."

Ryba L. Epstein
Advanced Placement instructor and College Board World History consultant

Jackie Tempo and the Ghost of Zumbi

Also by Suzanne Litrel

Jackie Tempo and the Emperor's Seal

Jackie Tempo and the Ghost of Zumbi

Suzanne Litrel

iUniverse LLC
Bloomington

Jackie Tempo and the Ghost of Zumbi

iUniverse books may be ordered through booksellers or by contacting:

iUniverse LLC
1663 Liberty Drive
Bloomington, IN 47403
www.iuniverse.com
1-800-Authors (1-800-288-4677)

Because of the dynamic nature of the Internet, any Web addresses or links contained in this book may have changed since publication and may no longer be valid. The views expressed in this work are solely those of the author and do not necessarily reflect the views of the publisher, and the publisher hereby disclaims any responsibility for them.

ISBN: 978-1-4401-7688-3 (sc)
ISBN: 978-1-4401-7687-6 (hc)
ISBN: 978-1-4401-7689-0 (e)

Printed in the United States of America

iUniverse rev. date: 09/19/2013

Acknowledgements

E. L. Doctorow once noted that "Writing a novel is like driving a car at night. You can see only as far as your headlights, but you can make the whole trip that way." My family and friends fuel me up and give me the green light to get going. Because of them, I know that the trip is worthwhile, and that I'm going to make it through.

A big thank you goes to Maddelena Padilla, Lisette Lors, and Aaron Johnson of the Bay Shore High School social studies department: I've so enjoyed our discussions – sometimes in between classes, during preps and after school – on trends and attitudes towards race and ethnicity in the Americas. You convinced me that this was a topic worth exploring in *The Ghost of Zumbi*. Dr. Frank Guridy, of the University of Texas at Austin, further enlightened me on this topic, and was very helpful regarding resources. Thank you for your patience!

To my AP World History friends, most of whom I've met at "Professor Camp", the Exam Readings in June, thank you for your constant support and super ideas. You mean "the world" to me! John Maunu, Laurie Mannino, Ryba Epstein, Linda Black, Michele Forman, Catherine Atwell, Pat Whelan, Jay Harmon, Ben Kahrl, David Dorman, Eric Hahn, Heidi Roupp – you are outstandingly gifted and giving teachers. With whom else would I discuss lesson plans at five o'clock in the morning on the way to the airport? Your effort and enthusiasm have inspired me to always try my best. The Long Island Council for Social Studies has also offered constant support. In particular, Gloria Sesso has been extraordinarily helpful and supportive.

The Ghost of Zumbi, though a work of historical fiction, was inspired in large part by my time in Brazil. My friends from Escola Graduada de São Paulo ("Graded"), which I attended from 1975 – 1983, have offered encouragement online – and at our recent high school reunion! The efforts of my Graded teachers have shaped my thinking: in particular, Mrs. Reeves, Mrs. Arnstein, Mr. Falls, Dr. Price, Mrs. Housel and Mrs. Dickinson pushed me to be a bit more reflective. Diane Finegan was kind enough to send me her terrific short stories; these really sparked my memory of life in Brazil.

To my Suigetsu Dojo 'family': we are a tight-knit group, and every single one of you has been wonderfully patient and supportive. Many thanks for your good cheer and friendship.

My own family has long been patient, understanding, helpful and truly amazing. My sisters Deborah Kloosterman, Carolyn Segalini, as well as my father Sandro Segalini, have only offered constant support.

To my dearest children: you are nothing if not brutally honest, and I am thankful that you both took the time to go over the story and tell me when to "liven it up" (Alec) and help me with chapter titles (Julia). To my husband Christopher, an avid reader whose keen eye has been critical in the writing of this story: you are my true north. You have long listened to my ramblings, parsed them for meaning, and then pointed me in the right direction. How could I ever be afraid of riding into the unknown, with you beside me?

This book is dedicated to the memory of Palmares and its brave defenders, who were very much "*um povo heróico*" – an heroic people.

Waiting is painful. Forgetting is painful.
But not knowing which to do is the worst kind of suffering.
—Paulo Coelho

Chapter 1:

Prisoners in Time

Brazilian jungle, 1783

"A sacrifice is offered, O Great One! Accept our humble gift!" The six-foot dancing mask drew closer, howling an unearthly tune.

All the red-haired woman could see was bare feet protruding from the bottom, feet that were marked by a few broken toenails, feet that had clearly covered a serious distance to get to this small clearing in the overgrown jungle. She willed herself to not look up; the imperfection of the feet was far less unsettling than the frozen grimace of the wooden mask, large as a shield and just as impenetrable. She sensed scrawny legs behind the mask and thought she could hear puffing, as the man who wore it struggled to keep going.

"I'm not afraid of you." With these words, the woman looked up. It was an interesting statement, particularly since she was tied to a stake, arms twisted around her back, feet roped together with the heaviest of cords.

The mask stopped, hovering two inches from her face. Now the woman was intensely aware that the crowd that encircled her from just a few feet away was holding its collective breath, waiting for the mask to make its next move. She choked down panic. She scanned the group of about a dozen of raggedly-dressed, barefoot runaway slaves, all very intent on what would happen next. The sun shone down on them in full force at that moment, and the woman squinted as sweat trickled into her eyes, unable to wipe it away.

Beyond the small clearing, the jungle was dark and silent; sunlight never pierced the heavy foliage that was home to myriad insects, reptiles, and other unimaginable creatures. Try as she might, the woman could not see beyond its dense screen. In spite of the mid-day heat, she shivered. She was being watched.

The mask drew back then, and the woman focused on the impassive face before her. She noticed the luster of its brightly painted lips, a marked contrast to the deadened black eyes that peered out at her. It spoke. "Pale fool."

This time, the woman recoiled in fear, nostrils flaring slightly. A light smattering of freckles stood out against her bleak face. The sun bore down on this odd group, illuminating them against the backdrop of the lush Brazilian jungle; a brightly colored bird flew overhead, cawing loudly as it arched against the sky. The man behind the mask raised a crudely-fashioned spear and danced closer to the bound woman; she twisted her head away as he leaned in towards her.

The crowd erupted in wild whoops and began to chant to a rhythmic beat, louder and louder still, until the woman saw only the flicker of torches and then the stark silhouette of tangled branches under a moonless sky. Just before she fainted, she locked eyes with the man behind the mask.

AUNT ISOBEL'S MANSION, PRESENT DAY

Precious autumn daylight filtered into a large, airy kitchen, burnishing the wooden floors to a deeper glow. As the day waned, Isobel Leroux's Brazilian housekeeper, Dona Marta, moved gracefully between the gourmet stove and tiled countertops, humming as she cooked the evening meal.

"The secret ingredient," said Dona Marta, smoothing her red-and-white checkered apron, and then checking that her shiny black hair was still piled high atop her head, "is you." She stirred the dark liquid, which was rapidly pulling away from the sides of the heavy skillet. It was dense by now, after five minutes of her care, and clung to the wooden spoon, hanging on as if for dear life.

"Me, Dona Marta?" Jackie Tempo stepped away from the stove to stare at the Brazilian housekeeper, whom she always addressed formally, as the woman was at least thirty years her senior. Still in her black running tights and oversized sweatshirt, she felt grungy next to

Dona Marta, who always seemed so well dressed and beautiful.

"Yes, *você*," Dona Marta replied, giving the wooden spoon a firm tap. Dark clumps fell out onto the rest of the mix. Jackie pushed a rebellious red curl away from her forehead and leaned over again, inhaling the rich aroma, dizzy as she looked at the chocolate confection in the pot.

"You see," Dona Marta continued, "when you cook, you breathe life into your food. You must pay attention, especially when a dish seems to be simple, like this one." She handed the spoon over to her young charge and motioned for her to continue stirring. "Or else ... if you are careless and hasty—"

"Tasty! That's right, it's gotta be tasty!" A tall, handsome young man ambled into the large, warm kitchen with a grin. He had also worked out after school, and wore old sweats and faded Led Zeppelin t-shirt. He pushed his shaggy brown hair out of his eyes, feigning wonder. "Wow! Want me to help?"

Jackie blushed and ducked her head. "The last time you 'helped' you ate half the *brigadeiros*!" It was true. Jon had nearly made himself sick by gorging on the cherry-sized, chocolate-sprinkled fudgy sweets.

Jon Durrie laughed. "Somebody's gotta do the dirty work!" He gave his friend a crooked grin. "Shouldn't I get something for driving you home?"

Jackie's blush deepened, and not for the first time, she wished her fair skin wouldn't betray her. She whirled around, fiery locks flying, and pretended to grab something from the ornately carved wooden cupboard. "Um, yeah. Whatever," the high school sophomore mumbled.

Dona Marta arched a brow and pursed her lips, suppressing a smile. "Is that how you talk to your friend?" She busied herself at the stove. "*Nossa Senhora!* How you young people talk these days!"

"Why are you crossing yourself now, Dona Marta?" Jon asked, smiling. He had learned from these after school visits that Dona Marta was in the habit of crossing herself and invoking God and the Virgin Mary. "She's a devout Catholic, like most Brazilians," Jackie had explained.

"*Nada, nada* – I mean nothing," the petite woman responded. "Jackie, fetch me some onions from the cellar, *por favor* – please."

Jackie slid off her stool and complied. She pulled open the large wooden door by the stove and disappeared down the steps to the cellar. Jon pretended not to watch her, but Dona Marta wasn't fooled.

"You must know, my dear, that I think you are the perfect gentleman," she addressed the high school senior, "and I expect you to behave as such." She raised a hand, dispelling Jon's protests before they left his lips. "As you know, Jackie is my employer's niece."

Dona Marta's employer, Isobel L'eroux, often traveled for her arts and antiques business. "So it is up to me, Anna Maria Beatriz Sousa de Marta, to make sure that the Jackie is safe." Dona Marta looked at Jon, who was a bit taken aback by this blunt turn of conversation.

"The poor child has lost both her parents in a terrible car crash," she continued, "and since she is under Isobel L'eroux's care, she is under *my* care, too," Dona Marta said fiercely, blinking back tears. She kissed the small gold cross that she always wore around her neck. "*Deus do Céu*," she prayed, "God in Heaven, please protect this child."

Jon had not realized how much Dona Marta loved Jackie, and hastened to reassure her. "OK, I understand – I want her to be safe, too."

Just then, Jackie reappeared at the top of the cellar stairs, hands full of onions, and closed the door most ungraciously with her backside. "These enough for you?" she asked Dona Marta, who was pretending to busy herself with the *brigadeiros*. The Brazilian woman just nodded.

"I'm sorry, Dona Marta, let me take this from you." Jackie eased the pot of gooey chocolate from the housekeeper's hands. Dona Marta smiled at the girl she loved like a daughter, and gave her a kiss on the cheek. Jackie returned the smile, composed now, and set the pot on the granite kitchen island. Jon clambered onto a stool opposite her and motioned for the bowl of rich chocolate goo.

"C'mon!" He lunged for the mixing bowl. "Let me have a go at it!"

Jackie swiped his hands away and continued mixing, straining as the stuff grew thicker. "All right," she conceded, "your turn. And no tasting!" She shoved the bowl across the counter and sat back on her stool, reflecting on how much had changed between them in so little time. Jon grinned, dark blue eyes sparking, pleased to have the sweet chocolate treasure to himself.

The last few weeks had been interesting, to say the least. Jackie and Jon had officially met when her aunt had hired him as a history tutor for Jackie. It seemed like a lifetime ago that Aunt Isobel had shown the two teens an ancient book from Samarkand, one of three, that had the power to transport its readers back in time.

Jackie sat back on her stool, thoughtful. "Do you know where they are?" she said in an undertone; they hadn't talked about their past adventure before, and she didn't want to scare Dona Marta with wild stories. When Jackie had opened the magic book - despite her aunt's protests - she and Jon were transported to Ming China, almost five hundred years ago.

"Yeah," Jon whispered, an eye on Dona Marta, who seemed to be mumbling yet another prayer as she fixed dinner. "Do you think about . . . where they are?" Jackie had found out that her parents were actually alive, but trapped in the past as they pursued Devon, Professor Tempo's former graduate student.

"They're trying to catch Devon." Jackie looked down to avoid Jon's steady gaze. Devon, it had turned out, was thrill-seeker who was more interested in living it up in the past than pursuing his graduate studies in the present. Jackie, Jon, and Aunt Isobel had managed to return here in Arborville, but Devon had escaped to another time – as did the Tempos, who were determined to bring him back in the present.

Dona Marta's back was to them now. Jon covered Jackie's hand with his own. "I know you miss them." He was referring to her parents.

"Yes," Jackie's voice quavered, but she caught herself and gave Jon a brave smile. After their adventure in China, she busied herself with clubs and sports, and threw herself into her schoolwork with a passion that astonished everyone, including herself. With the confidence of one who knows that the only thing that is important and real is the here and now, Jackie became fully immersed in the present. And besides, staying busy kept her mind off her worries.

"Great, so I'm out of a job," Jon had said half-ruefully, when she showed him a stellar grade on her last world history exam.

"Well, we'll see." Jackie had smiled, and glanced over at Aunt Isobel, who beamed at the grade. "This test was on Ming China, after all." And travelling back to Ming China may have given her a bit of edge.

Jackie's grades continued to improve dramatically, now that she was focused and willing to do schoolwork. While Jon was, in fact, relieved of his tutoring duties, they still saw each other in school. And when he found out that she had joined girls' cross-country, he began giving her a lift home. As captain of the boys' team, he was always one of the last out of the lockers, but she didn't mind waiting; she was grateful for the ride, and for his company. They never talked much about their adventure; it still seemed too bizarre to have happened.

For Jackie, at any rate, something had changed; where she had been distant and shy of her classmates when she first came to Arborville, she no longer worried about what they thought. Despite her involvement at school, she felt most at home curled up with a good read, losing herself in a story. The chatter of the girls at her locker struck her as banal, and while she was invited to many parties, she most often excused herself early, blaming an overbearing aunt. The reality was that Jackie had, in fact, suffered a deep loss. No matter how she looked at it, her parents were gone. This wasn't something she could really share.

"She's a fanatic when it comes to curfews," Jackie would lie about her aunt's strictness. Actually, Aunt Isobel was hardly ever home. At a prearranged time, Dona Marta would send their driver. Jackie, embarrassed by her aunt's enormous wealth, would meet him halfway down the block. At home, in bed with a great book, snug in flannel pajamas and warm sheets, Jackie would forget for a moment what had happened—what was happening—to her parents.

Jackie had no choice but to assume that her parents were safe and would make their way back home. She shook her head slightly as she watched Jon work the chocolate batter. *I just have to believe that everything will be okay*, she thought, *and then it will be.*

She looked up now at Dona Marta. "Aren't we done with this yet?" She and John had taken turns stirring the chocolate goo, and she pointed to what would become *brigadeiros*, their favorite Brazilian treat. Dona Marta nodded and reached for the bowl. Jon handed it over with not a little bit of reluctance.

"So now we see that the batter is firm, and we roll these up into little balls, like so." Dona Marta greased her clean hands with butter and rolled a perfect little sphere between her palms. "Then we dip it into the chocolate sprinkles, and then … this *doce*, this sweet is done. Wash your hands," she admonished the teens, who were already lunging for the goo. "First you eat dinner, then you may have the dessert."

Jon glanced at his running watch and jumped up. "Oh, man, I have to go. I forgot." He grabbed his keys and headed for the front door. "I'm sorry."

Jackie rushed after him, a perfect *brigadeiro* in hand. "Here—one for the road."

He was already out the front door. "No, gotta go, sorry," he said, but saw that Jackie blinked back a slight hurt. "But thanks," he mumbled and kissed her quickly on the head before ducking in his car and roaring out of the driveway. Jackie wandered back into the kitchen and put the lonely sweet on a plate.

Dona Marta turned off the stove and filled Jackie's plate with string beans, rice and *bife* steak, a thin pounded and fried slice of beef that she had seasoned well. Jackie plunked herself down at the counter, now set for one. Despite today's tough track workout, she wasn't so hungry. Dona Marta tempted her with *pão de queijo,* crispy balls of cheese.

"It was his turn to cook at home?" she inquired of Jackie.

"Right." Jackie nodded, pensive. Jon had sworn her to secrecy, but she had to tell at least one person that his mother was battling cancer, and was most of the time too weak from chemo treatments to do anything around the house. So Jon and his younger brother, Petey, divided up household chores, and preparing dinner was one of them. Petey, a sixth-grader, was usually responsible for set-up and clean-up, except for Fridays, which was pizza night—they were "off duty" then, and would eat right out of the box. Jackie wished Jon would open up some more, so that they could get help at home.

"At least tell Matt," she had urged him. Like everyone else in the high school, she referred to the school social worker by his first name. "He's cool, and he can probably find a way to help you guys out."

She had been down to The Dive, as the kids fondly called his cozy office in the high school, to see Matt and work out her own issues with her presumed dead—but now missing—parents. She loved the cramped room with its threadbare Persian rug warming up the white linoleum floor, books in every corner and crammed two deep on his bookshelves in an untidy, but organized fashion. "I know where everything is," he had growled at her when she suggested that she alphabetize his vast poetry collection. She had laughed then, because in spite of his heavy brows and menacing voice, there was no one in the world she felt safer with than the social worker/poet. While she couldn't tell Matt everything about her parents' real situation, he had helped her sort through her feelings as only a smart observer could.

But Jon would have none of it. He wouldn't talk to anyone except Jackie about his mom, and even then in the most abbreviated manner. He couldn't; his mother had made him promise not to. She was worried that she'd lose custody of the kids. Her ex-husband—Jon's father—was a highly successful but overbearing stockbroker who had never forgiven her for walking out on his oppressive ways. He was absolutely irate that Jon's mom had launched her own writing career and become fully independent of her ex. "You know your father thinks I'm a flaky writer. Well, this situation"—as she often referred to her cancer—"would lead to my losing you. I can take anything, but that would be too much to bear." And so Jon and his brother kept quiet for their mother's sake. But Jackie saw that they suffered, and she went out of her way to be nice to Petey.

Jackie picked at the food on her plate. She knew she needed to eat if she was to run well tomorrow, but after a few bites she put her fork down. "I'm sorry, Dona Marta. I guess I'm not that hungry after all. Can you save my plate for later?"

Dona Marta swooped the plate off the counter, frowning her disapproval. "*Va bem*," she assented, "all right, but for today only!" She covered the plate and tucked it into the enormous Sub-Zero refrigerator. Sighing, she wondered for the millionth time why Dona Isobel had such a glorious kitchen, since no one was around to enjoy her cooking except Wolfe, Jackie's big brute of a dog. She reached over to the built-in music system and with a deft flick of her wrist, the kitchen was filled with the soothing sounds of Brazilian music.

"*Vamos dançar*," Dona Marta hummed to herself, while Jackie helped her put the food away. "Yes, you'll get the leftovers … again," Dona Marta promised Wolfe, who looked at her adoringly. She marveled at how such a shaggy, ungainly hulk of a gray dog could have the eyes of an angel. Why did the beast love her so much? "Must be my natural culinary skill," she told Wolfe, scraping the leftovers into the dog's dish, "for I'm no Francis of Assisi." She crossed herself for mentioning the name of the revered saint and lover of all animals so lightly. "*Me desculpa*," she apologized, casting her eyes heavenward.

Just then the front door slammed. Jackie and Dona Marta looked at each other, startled.

"Jon?" Jackie called out. "Is that you …?"

Wolfe heard it first. He pricked his ears; barking wildly, he bolted from the room. Dona Marta reached for Jackie's hand and gripped it tightly. Suddenly, the house was filled with a strange, rhythmic beat. And then it came crashing down all around them like a great storm: the manic, insistent beating of drums.

"No, not now!" Jackie ran after Wolfe towards the great mansion's library.

Dona Marta clapped her hands over her ears and followed in breathless pursuit, and found the girl in the middle of the grand room.

Just then, the noise stopped.

And a book lay open on the middle of the glossy parquet floor.

"Oh, no." Jackie backed into Dona Marta. "I'm not going there again."

He who talks incessantly talks nonsense.
—African proverb (Ivory Coast)

Chapter II:

Waiting for Another Zumbi

Dona Marta bent down to pick up the book. "*Que interessante*," she murmured, "how interesting—a map of colonial Brazil." She felt strangely drawn to the old tome, with its worn binding and swirling designs. Funny that she had never seen it before; but then, this room held hundreds of strange volumes. It was nearly dark now, and she switched on an old-fashioned floor lamp, so she could read the title.

"*No!*" Jackie knocked the book out of her hand, and then picked it up in an instant. Dona Marta gasped in shock at the teen's violent action.

Jackie clutched the book against her chest. Her heart was pounding wildly, like the rhythm of the drums she thought she'd just heard. "I mean—I'm so sorry—but this book is … well, you can't touch it, for your own safety." They both glanced around the enormous room; the windows were locked, as were the large French doors.

Dona Marta pursed her lips, then took a deep breath and asked the Virgin Mary for patience under her breath. She had just opened her mouth to rebuke the pretty redhead when Jon's younger brother burst into the room.

"The front door was open, so …" Petey gulped. He was breathing heavily, and his light brown hair was plastered with sweat. Jackie noticed that his jeans seemed dirtier than usual, and he was wearing one of Jon's old t-shirts.

Jackie and Dona Marta looked at each other, confused. Hadn't they just heard it slam shut? A fierce wind rattled the library's window panes, and Jackie shivered as the Shangri-la Mansion groaned under the onslaught. This was a strange house, indeed. Aunt Isobel had always said it had a mind of its own. *She was right*, Jackie thought.

"So," Petey continued, his face ashen, "my mother is in the hospital. She just collapsed. Jon's in the ambulance with her, and I had to stay behind." The boy looked like he was going to collapse, too. "But I rode my bike here instead. Can you give me a ride, please?" he asked Dona Marta. "I've got to get there now." He glanced out the window; it was dark outside, and the wind was picking up.

"Of course, *meu amor*." Dona Marta enveloped the boy in a motherly hug, smothering him against her ample bosom. Petey was not used to such nurturing, and he choked back tears. "*Vamos*," said Dona Marta. "We will go now. Let us pray to give strength to your mother." She went back to the kitchen, removed her apron and hung it on a bronze peg by the stove. The dishes would have to wait. Then she reached out to Petey, who had followed without a thought. Jackie lingered in the library. Wolfe sensed that something was up. He whimpered slightly.

"You're in charge, boy," Jackie instructed her unsightly dog. He was a big, hairy beast whose matted fur was so scary no one had wanted to adopt him at the animal shelter. But as a six-year-old, Jackie had seen only Wolfe's true loving nature and begged her parents to take him home right then and there. From that time on, they were virtually inseparable.

She reached down to hug him; he was the last vestige of her old life with her parents. "Love you," she whispered, then added in her usual voice, "One sec, Dona Marta." With Wolfe was right on her heels, she ducked back into the library and hid the old book on a dusty lower shelf.

"Make sure no one messes with this." Wolfe sat right down in front of the shelf . He wagged his tail, looking for approval. "Good boy." Jackie hugged the dog once more. She glanced around the room; funny, she felt as if she were being watched. But Wolfe had settled on the shining parquet floor, guarding the room. No one else was here. Jackie shook her head, uneasy. Then she ran out of the room to catch up to the others.

BRAZILIAN JUNGLE, 1783

More than two hundred years back in time, deep in the jungles of Brazil, a pale man with colorless hair and watery eyes looked at the dancing figures in approval. He particularly liked their carved wooden masks and raffia outfits. In spite of the loud music that accompanied the shuffle of the dancers' feet, the red-haired woman remained slumped at the stake to which she had been tied.

"Yeah, this is my kind of party!" He fingered the beads at his neck, eyes darting over the scene. About a dozen runaway slaves danced in time to the beating of a mournful drum. "Can't we do some, you know, black magic? Get it—black?" He laughed again, this time a bit nervously. The proud African by his side did not respond, and Devon fell silent as he considered the formidable man beside him who had escaped from slavery only three days before.

"Well, then," said Devon, "you know that I'm a god, right? I mean—I freed you with my magic book." He waved a small text with odd markings at the African, who fell back a step. "You're not a slave anymore."

The black man glanced at him, arms crossed. Not for the first time, Devon considered the many scars on his back. Some were ridged, thick with scar tissue, forming angry red knots across his back; clearly, the man had been fiercely whipped many times. It was just as evident, however, that his spirit had not been broken.

"Yes, funny little white man"—Devon bristled at these words, but the man continued—"I will grant that you have divine powers." The powerfully muscular African stood his ground, eyes flashing. Devon was fascinated by the whiteness of his eyes and teeth. "But I am a prince, and you know that I belong with my people." He locked glances with Devon, who was by now feeling a bit uneasy, in spite of the very special book he had bound tightly to his chest, tucked away in his shirt. "So what is this … dance? This custom is very odd—those people are from a tribe I do not know."

The unlikely pair stared at the chanting African dancers and the pale red-haired woman.

"Right," Devon agreed. "I taught them those rituals myself, from my special book of wisdom. But she"—he pointed to the white woman—"is one of my kind, and she is being punished."

The African shrugged. He had seen more misery in the last year than he had ever thought possible. And all because of white men, it seemed. What did it matter if one of their own tribe suffered? He closed his eyes against the violent images seared in his memory. It was no use. He needed to take action, now. Perhaps that would make him forget.

"Take me to my people," he repeated, staring at Devon. He had heard of a *quilombo*, a runaway slave community, deep in the jungles of Pernambuco. While the *quilombo* welcomed most runaways, including Indians and mestizos, he had been told that it was run by true Angolans. These were his people.

Devon, too, was searching for what he hoped were hidden kingdoms deep within the Brazilian jungle. He had read that from Bolivia to St. Domingue, from Pernambuco to Alagoas, communities of runaway slaves in Spanish and Portuguese America offered hope to those who remained behind and toiled at the mercy and whim of cruel masters.

Palmares, the most notorious of these *quilombos*, was a particular symbol of hope. At one point, it was rumored to have held up to twenty thousand runaways and free-born Africans, Indians, mestizos, and mulattoes. Highly organized and militaristic, Palmares was a thorn in the side of the Brazilian government for over one hundred years. Neither the efforts of Dutch mercenaries nor the Brazilian government were able to destroy Palmares completely. And so generations had lived in freedom until the end of the seventeenth century, when Palmares was destroyed by broken promises and an ultimate betrayal.

It had been said that the survivors of the *quilombo* sought refuge deeper in the *mato*, the jungle, where the descendants of Palmares lived out their lives quietly— but always in fear. *Waiting for another Zumbi.* Devon's lip curled at the thought of Zumbi, the fearless *quilombo* leader who had died coming to the aid of a friend. When the friend betrayed him to the Portuguese, Zumbi had been killed on the spot, and his head was paraded around the town of Recife for days. But the memory of Zumbi lived on, and plantation masters worried; the trickle of runaways had not ceased.

Devon would lead them to greatness. Armed with knowledge gleaned from the twenty-first century, and guided by his mysterious, time-traveling text from the past, he would be their savior. And he would lead the greatest army ever known to man and would rule over all of lush Brazil.

Transfixed by the scene before him, Devon whispered, "Oh, I will take you to your people. I will."

One who does not look ahead remains behind.
—Brazilian proverb

CHAPTER III:

RUN AWAY

AUNT ISOBEL'S MANSION, PRESENT TIME

"Just watch your step, dearest. The woods are quite tricky this time of year," Aunt Isobel called out to Jackie as she handed off her bags to her longtime butler, who was surprisingly strong, for one well into his seventies. She had just returned from one of her fantastic voyages. "Oh, I have a most unusual rug for your room, my dear. When you return from your run, let's look at the patterns together."

"Thank you, James." Isobel L'eroux bestowed a dazzling smile on the butler as he staggered under the weight of her luggage and patted her thick white bun into place. He gave a curt nod and glared at the redhead who sat on the marble floor of the grand rotunda entrance to her aunt's mansion, aptly named Shangri-La for the mythical paradise.

"Excuse me, miss." She was in his way.

Jackie smiled up at him. She knew that he didn't like her very much. "What a young whippersnapper! The girl should be grateful to her aunt – she could be scrubbing dishes this very minute!" she had overheard him tell Dona Marta. The butler and the housekeeper argued endlessly about Jackie's behavior. He thought the teenager a rude, messy thing too immersed in books; the Brazilian would hotly defend the child, calling James a cold fish.

"No problem, James!" Jackie scooted aside and hid a smile as the butler made his way past her, mumbling under his breath. She knew it irritated him to think that she was related to the one of the most illustrious figures in the field of antiques, Isobel Leroux. Her aunt had the great auction houses of Sotheby's and Christies's at her beck and call; just last week, Vogue magazine camped out at Shangri-la to do a major photo shoot of Aunt Isobel at home. James was in a snit, worried about Jackie getting in the way, all the while mumbling that she should have been shipped off to a finishing school instead of sullying Shangri-la.

"Ah. . . what a day!" Aunt Isobel breathed in rapture. "It's good to be home." With a brilliance peculiar to clear winter mornings, light streamed over them from the sparkling windows in the domed ceiling of the foyer. Everything in the room was thrown into sharp relief. It was a glorious day, and Jackie looked forward to her run. "Please be careful," she warned her niece again.

Jackie grinned up at her aunt as she flung out a leg and stretched. "I know my way around by now." The boys' and girls' cross-country teams made good use of Whispering Woods, so-called for the rustling maples that encouraged their efforts on the miles of hills and trails of the famous nature preserve. Shangri-La abutted the Woods, which many on the team swore were haunted. Coach joked that it made them run faster, and indeed, no one lingered over workouts in the Woods.

Except for Jackie. Now that the cross-country season was over, she still hit the trails on the weekends; she was always restless, and running forced her into the present, away from anxiety about her parents. When her aunt protested that a young girl shouldn't run alone through a forest, Jackie pointed out that the last assault in Arborville had been in town—and that was during the Great Depression, when the mayor was caught stealing cash from the town vault in the middle of the night. Not much had happened since then in this sleepy New England town, except that many young people had moved away, looking for better opportunities elsewhere, lured by the promise of Providence or Boston.

"Anyway," Jackie reminded Aunt Isobel, "Wolfe will come with me." At the sound of his name, Wolfe uncoiled himself from a corner of the vast living room and quickly maneuvered his way through the many antiques.

Jackie jumped up and gave her aunt a hug, then stepped back to fully appreciate the woman's latest outfit.

Aunt Isobel was not known in town for her trendy sense of style. But she was absolutely lovely, short and slightly plump, she had a distinct way of dressing that attested to her keen interest in other cultures. While her pure white hair was always swept up in a high bun, her fashion changed almost daily. Today, back from another trans-Atlantic voyage of rare art discovery, she wore a long, flowing, multicolored print; a matching bandana was wound around her head. Fine-boned and delicately featured, Aunt Isobel reminded Jackie of an exotic bird.

"See you in a bit. Can't wait to see the rug," said Jackie, ignoring the concern in Isobel's amethyst eyes as she headed for the door, Wolfe in tow. A blast of frigid air slammed the door shut.

"C'mon, boy, let's go," Jackie urged her mutt, who had caught a scent at the base of an ancient oak and was rooted to the spot. Wolfe's nose twitched as he processed all the information the tree had to give him. Jackie jogged in place, impatient. "Come *on!*"

The ungainly dog bounded ahead with a grace that belied his awkward-looking body, and Jackie settled into a rhythm behind him. She smiled slightly, recalling her father's frustration with the dog, who lost all control when he picked up a scent. "I swear he's got beagle in him … somewhere!" her dad would say. The thought of it made Jackie laugh, as Wolfe was a large dog by any measure. Even so, when he shot after a rabbit, it would be hours before he returned, panting heavily, collapsing on their porch, glad for the experience of a good chase. Still, David Tempo would worry—not about the leash laws in their university neighborhood, which he considered silly and excessive—but for the safety of his dog, his "favorite son," as Jackie and her mom would joke.

A lifetime ago, Jackie thought, as she ran through the forest, picking her way along the trail, skipping over gnarled roots partially hidden by the autumn leaves. The chill of late fall was partially blunted by bright sunshine, and she relaxed into a steady pace. Ahead of her, Wolfe bounded over a fallen tree that directly blocked their path, and she followed suit, clearing the trunk with an ease that surprised her. She landed softly on the other side and began a quick ascent towards the Bluffs. *Go*, she urged herself, *go. Up*. Images, unbidden, flashed before her and were erased with every sure step. Her parents, in the old house; her father, on a ship off the coast of China; Aunt Isobel, in the rotunda; Jon, in the kitchen last night, lunging for the *brigadeiros*; Petey, badly frightened, who had come with them after all to the hospital; their mother, stabilized for now, tubes sticking in her arms, shooing them all away; Jon again, this time running by her, teasing.

Her heart skipped a beat, and then her world dwindled to the immediate: a large stone in the path, a thick patch of fallen leaves, the twisting way along the Bluffs, the roar of the Atlantic Ocean on her right, a quick drop down and now a scramble up, forward, always, one foot in front of the other. This was why she loved to run: it was that simple. And everything else was so … complicated. *Just go*. She could taste the salt in the air, and it seemed to her that it tasted like freedom. And she was flying now, over roots, over rocks, feet light and sure. She was breathing hard, a pain she embraced, knowing that it meant that she was alive and in the present, and still she pushed herself on, up the last hill, and into the light.

Much silence makes a powerful noise.
—African proverb

CHAPTER IV:

DOCUMENT BASED QUESTIONS

ARBORVILLE HIGH SCHOOL, PRESENT TIME

"All the information that you need is in the book."

Jackie leafed through the worn volume from the back of her history classroom and stared at the in-class assignment before her. Ms. Thompson's clear voice still rang in her ears, and she looked up to see her teacher humming quietly, absentmindedly spinning an old-fashioned desk globe with her left hand and grading papers with her right. Music was very much a part of their class experience, as was art and literature. "What do you hear?" Ms. Thompson would ask as they listened to a particular song. "What's the mood of the music? What is the composer trying to tell us?"

Aunt Isobel had attended Meet the Teacher night and very much appreciated Ms. Thompson's approach to learning history. "Artists are a direct connection to the times—they are the soul of an era," she proclaimed in approval. "The cultural lens is the clearest of them all. Artists are our window to the world."

On this cold November afternoon, the only music in Ms. Thompson's history class was in Jackie's head, a hypnotic beat that they'd listened to the class before. This past week they were studying the cultural effects of the trans-Atlantic slave trade. "How can the human spirit endure such terrible physical and emotional oppression?" Ms. Thompson had asked the class. "When one is in shackles, is it possible to be free?" These questions had led to an intriguing discussion on the nature of freedom, as one of the students pointed at one of the many quotations scattered on the walls throughout Ms. Thompson's room: "Man is born free, but everywhere is in chains." Ms. Thompson had then asked the class for whom that quote, written by French Enlightenment thinker Rousseau, was really intended? Did it apply to women? African slaves?

Then the class had gone on to examine the rich culture of colonial Brazil, where most of the Angolan slaves had mixed their native culture with that of the Portuguese. With a half hour to go in the ninety-minute period, the class was given a packet of documents to examine and interpret. Ms. Thompson wanted the students to add information not directly found in the packet, so they were allowed to use notes and the books at the back of the room for extra detail.

Jackie loved settling into work after an exciting discussion, her head buzzing with ideas. She especially liked the fact that her teacher had given them a head start on their homework, to be handed in at the next class. Book on her lap, packet on the desk, she bent over the intriguing documents and began to interpret them.

She quickly dispensed with a short document on the sale of African slaves, shuddering to think of the heartless process. She didn't want to linger on such pain. Though she loved history, there were parts that were almost too difficult to bear; how could people be so cruel?

Turning to the next document, a pen-and-ink drawing of what appeared to be some sort of religious ritual dance, she carefully examined the large masks, legs emerging from behind the intricately carved faces fringed with raffia. But Jackie suddenly had trouble focusing and felt intensely uncomfortable. Her arms were covered in goose bumps; she pulled down the sleeves of her sweater and wrapped her arms around herself as if for protection. She glanced out the window, and not for the first time, thought about Jon. Then she drew her unruly long curls into a tight, high ponytail to help her focus, and stared at the drawing. *Think!*

Still, her eyes glazed over. The room was annoyingly hot—as usual, the heat was going full blast, and the windows were slightly stuck and couldn't be opened properly. She glanced up from her paper and around the room, at posters of African and Latin American art, and at the quotations posted in strategic locations. The one on the door, from Nietzsche, was her favorite:

"That which does not kill you makes you stronger." In fact, many of the kids complained that Thompson was trying to kill them with her demanding assignments, but Jackie understood that they were slowly turning into historians and writers, whether they liked it or not.

It was unnervingly quiet in the room. Ms Thompson had stopped humming and was leaning over an essay, mouth pursed. She made a few notes on the paper. Jackie shifted in her chair, feeling strangely ill at ease.

The teen pushed an errant red lock out of the way and sighed. *Concentrate*, she willed herself. But while history was her favorite class—apart from English—she felt an overwhelming need to run out of the room. She flipped to the front of the packet and reread the main question.

To what extent did the trans-Atlantic slave trade affect culture in Africa and the Americas? she read for what seemed like the hundredth time. She flipped back to the document with the giant dancing masks and sighed as she tried to figure out what the scene had to do with the question.

"What do you see?" Ms. Thompson addressed the whole class. She had put down her pen, and looked around at her students thoughtfully. "Remember to start with what's in front of you. *Then* analyze for meaning." This was normally one of Jackie's favorite activities; she loved to examine artwork or documents for content and meaning. Sometimes they'd spend the whole class period on just one piece, discussing the artist, the message, and the times—and secret messages within the work that the artist conveyed to audiences beyond his or her immediate patron.

Twenty-five heads bowed over their work again as Ms. Thompson quietly made her rounds. Jackie stole another look at her teacher as she made her way down the rows of desks. She was tall and graceful; her long dark hair was pinned up in a casual twist. Jackie knew that she taught yoga outside the classroom, and had once been a professional ballet dancer until injuries forced her to stop. It was she who had encouraged Jackie to go out for the cross-country team. "We need to channel that restless spirit of yours," she'd said. Surprisingly, Ms. Thompson was single, and for the better part of the year, the other girls in the class had been contriving to set her up with the new foreign language teacher, Mr. Havel. But as far as anyone knew, nothing had happened between the brilliant beauty and the Czech-born French teacher, in spite of the countless fake love notes the girls in room 266 sent across the hall to Mr. Havel's room.

Jackie sighed. If only it were that easy to fix another's destiny. If only the world could be as she willed it. In a perfect world, Ms. Thompson and Mr. Havel would be together; her parents would be back; and they'd all live in Arborville, now that she'd come to like it, because Jon …

Shaking her head, she willed herself back to the present and squinted at the document, as if that would make it all the more clear. She absently noted a tiny figure tied to some sort of ceremonial pole.

Then she froze.

There on the page, caught in another time and place, was her mother.

He who asks questions cannot avoid the answers.
—African proverb

CHAPTER V:

⊕N THE R⊕AD AGAIN

Jackie started abruptly and gasped in shock. She brought the document packet right up to her eyes.

There was her mother, all right. While the picture was in pen and ink, the details were so exquisite that she could make out the very lashes that ringed her mother's eyes. Her hair, long and curly like Jackie's, was slightly frizzy and unkempt. Her eyes were wide; it seemed to Jackie that she stared beyond the paper right at her, her mouth open in surprise. Her arms were twisted around the back of a stake, and her legs were tied together at the bottom.

Jackie choked out loud. At that very moment, Anthony Milano decided to come to her rescue, and thumped her on the back—hard.

"You okay, doll?" Anthony fancied himself a latter-day leading man; he certainly dressed the part. His pin-striped shirtsleeves were rolled up to reveal strong forearms; his black silk vest gleamed beneath the fluorescent classroom lights. He leaned in close, eyes full of concern. "Seriously, baby, talk to me."

In spite of herself, Jackie rolled her eyes. She and Anthony were good friends, though his initial introduction had been a bit odd—"You're not my type, but I can tell a sharp cookie when I see one. Got last night's homework on ya?" He was the first to make her feel welcome at Arborville High School. In fact, they usually ate lunch together—"Mind if I join ya? The guys are afraid I'll take their women"—and Jackie had come to enjoy his droll, outdated commentary.

But not now. Jackie shook her head and squeezed her eyes shut. Ms. Thompson hurried to her desk, eyebrows arched in concern.

"I'm fine," Jackie muttered. "No, I mean, I'm actually not." She pushed her chair back and it toppled over. Ms. Thompson reached out to help her, but the bell rang and Jackie darted out of the room, leaving Anthony and their teacher standing in confusion.

"What can I say, except—women, ya know?" Anthony winked at Ms. Thompson and slung his backpack over his shoulder, joining the stream of kids who were leaving the room. Ms. Thompson shook her head, puzzled, and greeted the students who were coming in.

Jackie bolted from the room in a panic, too stunned to think straight, but too frozen to talk. She ran smack into Jon, who was waiting outside the classroom. He seemed paler than usual, and was fiddling with the worn strap of his grey backpack.

"Look," she blurted out, shoving the document packet right at him.

Jon stepped back, irritated. He'd had a rough night at the hospital, and Petey was a mess over their mother. "So? What do you want from me?" He pushed his shaggy dark hair out of his eyes and frowned. He didn't have time for this.

"Here!" Jackie jabbed a finger at the last document. She looked up at him expectantly.

"What?" he exclaimed. "Just tell me!" His jaw tightened as he looked down at the petite redhead.

As throngs of kids heading for lunch pushed past, Jackie started to hyperventilate, drawing deep, nervous gulps of air. She stumbled back against a locker, clutching the documents to her chest.

"Whoa, whoa … let's get out of here." Jon put a steady hand on her shoulder and steered her toward the door.

Outside, the air was bracing, and Jackie's eyes watered against the cold. She curled her fingers inside her green striped sweater and wrapped her arms around her for warmth. Jon stared down at the packet, frowning.

"Who"—Jackie took her time now, trying to steady her voice—"who does the woman in document five look like?"

Jon shrugged. "I don't know, this is a weird picture." He held it back a bit. "It's funny, but"—he looked up down at Jackie for a second and then back at the drawing— "she actually looks a lot like you."

"Right." Jackie nodded. The freezing air made her nose start to run. "You're looking at my m-mother." She was starting to feel dizzy again.

Jon's jaw dropped; he recovered just as quickly. "Okay, then, let's go." He pulled Jackie to the parking lot. "We better find out what's going on."

They clambered into his old Buick, but the engine didn't take when he tried to turn on the ignition. "Not the time to act up, Christine." It was a battered blue vehicle he'd picked up for a song. It was in such bad shape inside that the seat lining had worn away. With the foam padding exposed, he'd resorted to pulling old T-shirts over the seat backs.

Jackie always thought it weird that he'd named it for some psycho car in a Stephen King novel. "What if it really freaks out on you?" she'd asked. "Nah, not if she's treated right." Jon had read every Stephen King novel out there—and there were many—and said it was his nod to the prolific author's greatness. Jackie, however, suspected that it had more to do with Jon's desire to escape the very difficult reality of his life, which was certainly what she wanted to be doing right now. The image of her mother tied to a stake was fixed in her mind. She had to help her—now. She gulped and squeezed her eyes shut. *Please, Christine*, she said silently to the car. *Just go.*

Jon must've read her mind. For once, he was short with the old junk heap he called a car. "Let's *go*, already!" He smacked the dashboard in frustration, and the car finally came to life. He put a hand on

Jackie's battered car seat and looked over his right shoulder as he backed up.

"Coast is clear," he announced. He sounded almost brave.

Jackie didn't need to ask where they were going.

One must talk little and listen much.
—African proverb

CHAPTER VI:

THE LIVING GHOST

"How very disgusting. Like the underbelly of a snake." A small, dark hand reached out and poked the white thing.

"No—more like a worm!"

"Out!" The little hand was slapped away by Elva, the medicine woman, and the two children ran out together to the edge of the clearing, more shaken by what they had seen than by the scolding of the most powerful person in the *quilombo*.

The best friends had finished their morning's work; Beatriz had ground her share of manioc, and Pedro had collected enough twigs for two days. They had been playing by Elva's hut, when they peeked in and saw a strange red-haired being crumpled on the packed dirt floor, a thin cloth covering its inert form.

Elva had come upon them then and angrily shooed them away. "*Para fora*! Get out!" Her age was a subject of much debate among all the children; what was not arguable, however, was the fact that she was a fearsome being. Though she was clearly quite old, her wiry white hair framing her head like an electric halo, Elva stood straight-backed, light blue eyes shining from within a very dark face that was strangely smooth and unlined. Everyone knew she had secret potions that could transform her enemies into spiders and snakes; it was also known that her breath could bring a dead man back to life—if his spirit were willing. There were whispers as well that she was several hundred years old. She kept mostly to her hut and to her secret paths in the jungle, but when she strode through the *quilombo*, everyone bowed down to her, for they knew her power was immense. Although she had the face of a young woman, one had only to look at her wrinkled hands and her hair, shot through with white, to know the truth: that she held the secrets of the ages, and her magic protected them all from the white slavers of Brazil.

"She is as old Mother Earth herself," Pedro whispered to Beatriz. "I bet she was even in Palmares." Pedro himself was only seven, four years junior to Beatriz's eleven. He liked to impress her. Anyone over ten years of age had an air of authority that only double digits could bestow. Of course, any adult—especially Elva—was positively ancient. "Right?" Pedro pressed on.

Beatriz nodded, pensive. It was possible. Their own mothers had been quite young when they came to this runaway slave community deep in the interior of Brazil.

That was nearly twelve years ago, and the *quilombo* was well established at that time.

"It is possible," nodded Beatriz. She was a light-skinned mulatto with golden eyes and full lips. Taller and thinner than the others, she was known as Queitinha, or "Little Quiet One." Her father, she was told, was a Dutch scholar who had fallen hard for her mother. He had tried to take Anande as his legal wife, but the Dutch mission refused to recognize the sanctity of their union. Apparently the Dutch were horrified by the love Pieter van der Roos felt for the dark Angolan slave. In the end, they carted him off, screaming for his only true love, on the first ship back to Holland. "He'll come to his senses once he lays eyes on a blonde woman again," the leading Dutch emissary had snorted. But he was wrong. Pieter threw himself off the ship the first chance he got—and that was just off the coast of Recife, in shark-infested waters. The Dutch elders in their dark frocks had winced and turned away, not daring to imagine the fate that befell him.

Anande, a striking girl of royal lineage, found herself with child not soon after. From what she had seen of this deceptive paradise called Brazil, she knew what that meant: her child, a being created from love, would be taken from her arms upon full weaning, never to be seen again. Dark as she was, and straight out of Africa, it would never have been possible for Anande to wed Pieter outright.

"And so," Anande had told her only daughter, Beatriz, many times, "I did the only thing possible. I ran looking for a place like Palmares, the most famous *quilombo* of them all."

"But weren't you afraid?" This was a story of which Beatriz never tired. "Of the jungle, of the beasts?"

Anande would smile. "No, treasure of my heart, child of my mothers. I knew that as long as you had taken root inside of me, I had the courage to find freedom for us both. I would find freedom, because you insisted on it. Your spirit has always been strong, *meu amor*," she would say, mixing Portuguese in with her native language, "and I knew there had to be a way."

And so Anande had traveled through the interior— the land away from the Brazilian coastline—to the west, deep into the Serra do Barriga—the mountain of the belly, as it was called—where they would be safe. She moved by night, using the ancient sight of her ancestors' ancestors and the songs of her grandmothers to comfort her as she moved slowly, deliberately, heavy with child, looking for a safe place to give birth. Her daughter would be born free.

Everyone back in Pernambuco knew that other *quilombos* had sprung up since Palmares was dismantled. The *mestres dos engenhos*, masters of plantations, were angry that they had to keep an excessively watchful eye on their fresh slaves, who were the ones most likely to bolt. This was certainly true of Anande, who had been at her master's house for less than a year when she left, pregnant with Beatriz. She would not deliver her child into slavery, even if the risk of capture meant death for them both. More than a few people wondered if Beatriz's quiet nature was connected to her mother's silent flight from captivity. Any noise would have meant capture. And so Anande had given birth alone, deep in the forest, biting down on a stick to keep from screaming as she endured the worst of her labor pains.

But where Beatriz was quiet and refined, Pedro was loud and rambunctious. Even in a *quilombo* of this size, his comings and goings were heralded by shouts (his own) and still more shouts (his mother's).

"You are getting ready for your first passage of life," she would tell him, reminding him that the time was at hand where he would be temporarily secluded with those of his age, in partial preparation for manhood. "Just like in our ancestral home," Pedro's mother would say, caressing his soft hair. "One day you will be a man, and it is here that you will reach adulthood according to our custom." Then she would slap him in the head, to show evil spirits that she didn't care for him all that much.

Which, of course, she did. She anguished over his Portuguese name—Pedro—and wished he had been named by the village chief rather than the master of the *engenho*, the plantation from which she had run away. She couldn't bear that her son carried the same name as that cruel man. Then again, Pedro meant "rock" in Portuguese, and this certainly described the state of his thick skull. She liked to remind him of that.

At any rate, it was he, Pedro "the Rock," who tried to drag Beatriz back into the medicine woman's hut.

"Let's go see that white person again!" he whispered excitedly. He could not believe what he had seen—she was so incredibly pale, beyond ugly. "Imagine that, a person with color only in her hair and eyes! Maybe she's a living ghost!" Pedro hopped excitedly about, coal-black eyes sparkling at the thought. "Maybe she can tell us about our ancestral home!"

"Quiet down!" At the next hut over, a woman was nursing a sleepy baby. She glared at the troublemaker.

Just then, Pedro's mother came storming down the beaten path and yanked him away by the ear. "'Living ghost!' I'll show you a living ghost—when I'm through with you!" Oblivious to his howls, she dragged her son back home.

Beatriz watched them with all the seriousness of an eleven-year-old keeping a very big secret, suppressing a smile as she heard Pedro's mother threaten him with women's work if he didn't behave.

Then she heard the most frightening moan. She stepped up to the open window in spite of herself. Shivering at the sight before her, she took a faltering step back and stumbled on a small rock.

"Who's there?" Elva's clear voice rang out once more and reached to the very center of Beatriz's being.

The girl gathered herself up and ran away.

If you know your history/ Then you would know where you are coming from
coming from
—Gilberto Gil

Chapter VII:

Between Worlds

Elva stood at the entrance to her hut with a fearsome scowl on her face, muttering angrily at the disappearing child. Then she turned to tend her pale patient, who was stirring now on the dirt floor.

"What is this place?" Judith Tempo could barely speak; her voice was hoarse. *As if I hadn't used it for centuries*, she thought ruefully, catching the medicine woman's eye. The older woman squatted beside her, grinding something into fine powder. She muttered to herself, and her garbled speech was punctuated with sharp cries.

Beatriz should have known not to peer inside the hut; this was forbidden, and on one occasion when she had done so, some years before, she had regretted it deeply, wishing to erase the awful sight forever. Still, the young girl had always felt strangely close to Elva, and deep down inside, wished the old woman would notice her.

That she did. When Elva had called out, Beatriz quickly dropped down and snuck a short distance away. But she had crept back to the hut and squatted a few paces away, tracing swirling designs on the dirt with a thin twig. A feeling of peace came over her as she repeated the patterns again and again. All would be well. Elva was not only the *quilombo's* medicine woman, but also its *orixá*, or high priestess. As such, she could cast the strongest of spells on all who dared to cross her path. She could see into the past and future, with the magic she had learned when she was chosen by her predecessor. She also had the gift of healing, and Beatriz felt certain that Elva would cure whatever ailed the strange-looking white woman.

Elva mixed a few drops of liquid into the powder, and then scraped it out of the bowl with a fine silver spoon. "Eat this," she told Judith, looking into the white woman's eyes for the first time. She did not flinch at the strange shade of green, but gazed deep into the other woman's soul. Judith stared back at the medicine woman's shining eyes. Somehow, she trusted her. She held out her hand for the spoon, and choked down the horrid stuff with a slight wince. Then she returned the shiny spoon, with its ornate handle, to its owner.

Satisfied, Elva wiped the spoon on her skirt. "Many moons ago, our spirits were guided to this sacred space," she began. "We knew not where we were running to, but only what we were running from … a life of unspeakable tragedy and pain beyond this world. And it is here, as in the great Palmares, that we have found our voices and ourselves once again. Everyone who comes here has run away from terrible misfortune. We follow the traditions of our Angolan ancestors, but respect any—African, Indian, mestizo, mulatto, or even a white person like yourself—who have come seeking shelter. So you are safe from those who would have bound and hurt you."

Judith reached for the old woman's hand. "I thank you. I do understand what it's like to be tossed about from one place to another, but"—she searched the medicine woman's face—"I can't even begin to imagine the horrors you've escaped."

The former slave nodded. "No, you cannot." Her eyes fell on the strange book by Judith's side. It glowed, and the strange, swirling patterns seemed to move before their eyes. Judith took in Elva's curiosity and placed the book in front of her.

"I have never seen such a thing," said the old woman. She sat back and poked it with a long fingernail. "It is shaped like a box. What makes it so powerful? Does it contain secrets?" Elva looked up at her strange guest, curious.

"In a way. Books tell stories," Judith explained. "Sometimes they reveal truths that are difficult to bear, and sometimes they take you—"

"Into the past—or the future?" Elva said softly. "But how can a book speak to you?" She picked up the volume with its strange swirling designs. "I do not hear it. Do you?" She held the book to her ear. "Nothing."

"Yes," Judith acknowledged, "it's true that the book itself doesn't talk. But when we see the symbols inside, which form words and have meaning, then we can say that the book speaks to us." She tilted her head thoughtfully. "It's very different from the way your people have preserved the stories from the past, isn't it?"

The white-haired woman nodded. "Yes," she said. "In our tradition we have griots, storytellers chosen at a young age to share with our tribes the wisdom of our ancestors. In this way our heritage is preserved, and our culture is shared by all who listen." Elva tapped the book. "This must be a very lonely way of learning stories, because only one person at a time can experience what the book has to say."

Judith smiled. "Oh, you're never alone when you have a good book with you."

"But do all your people read the symbols that reveal the stories? Do all your people share the same books?" Elva persisted. "Are there some without? Who creates these books? Are there truths that are distorted? Are there stories that have been hidden, that are not permitted to be shared? If one does not possess a book, does that mean he is ignorant of your culture and traditions? Have you no storytellers that reveal truths to many people at once? Or must a person go off alone, with a … book to gain understanding?"

Judith had no simple response for the medicine woman, who had lived in this runaway community all her life and obviously had no experience with books. Still, as an historian, she did her best to explain.

"I know some things about your culture, things no one shared with me personally, but that I learned from a book," she said. "For instance, I know that the African griots told mostly epic stories, like that of Sundiata." Elva's eyes gleamed in recognition at the mention of the famous king. "I know that in your culture, ancestry is traced through the mother, so people recite their lineage from their mother's side." Elva nodded. "I also know of the terrible slave trade that has brought your people from very far away, across a vast body of water, to work on plantations, sometimes to the death." Judith paused. "But I've read much of that knowledge for myself, in books. In this way so much information can be shared, with so many people, in many different places."

Deep in the jungle, a bird called out, the harshness of its cry shattering the sleepiness of the *quilombo*. The trees rustled, then all was quiet again.

"Tell me more of these books," Elva ordered.

So Judith continued with her story. She spoke of her father's bookstore in Ann Arbor, Michigan, and of how she and her sister Isobel grew up among the rare volumes—dusty portals to other worlds. She told of the appearance of a mysterious crate that smelled like sandalwood and faraway places. It contained three strangely marked books from Samarkand. Judith's voice dropped as she revealed how she and Isobel had discovered that the books could literally transport them out of time and place, reading the owner's intentions, and serving as translator and guide. The problem, she explained, was in getting back.

"It was our secret, until one of my husband's students stole one of these rare books, and started traveling back and forth in time. We've been trying to find him ever since. He's an unscrupulous young man—some would say evil—bent on power and will stoop as low as it takes to get what he wants." She didn't add her worst fear: that Devon might use his keen understanding of history to disrupt its course.

Elva looked deep into Judith's eyes; it was as if she was scanning her very soul. The high priestess reached out an ancient finger and touched her pale forehead, then asked, "What about your daughter?"

Judith shivered; she had not yet spoken of Jackie. She bowed her head, choking back hot tears. "She's lost to me for now, somewhere in the future. That's all I can tell you about her right now."

"Yes," Elva said slowly, "what you say is true." She nodded, and her eyes glazed over for an instant, then came into sharp focus. "I myself have traveled between worlds, to places past; I have seen the future. Tell me … of your world as it is, and of the places and times you have visited."

Judith knew that she should just start at the beginning, whatever that was. She sensed they were waiting, but for what? No matter. They had time. She was going nowhere—for now. So she began with her own life story.

"Once upon a time—but many years ago —a girl was born in a little town far, far away …"

Deep in the heart of the thick Brazilian jungle, the red-haired woman and the high priestess quietly exchanged stories through a long and humid night. A girl of eleven, remarkable in her beauty, stretched and stood watch outside their hut. Trancelike, she drew strange designs on the ground, and then curled up by the door again.

Not far away, a mighty Angolan prince sought to reclaim his kingdom, thousands of miles from his ancestral home. Dogging his steps was a cunning traitor from another time who pursued his own dreams of ill-gotten grandeur.

And centuries ahead, a trembling teen raced to rescue her mother from a terrible scene of death and destruction. In a grand old library she reached for a book that was bound by the same hypnotic patterns the young Beatriz was tracing in another time.

Be brave. Take risks. Nothing can substitute [for]experience.
—Paulo Coelho

CHAPTER VIII:

TIME TRAVELS

"I know it has to be here somewhere," Jackie half muttered to herself as she scanned the spines of the many books in her aunt Isobel's library. "Where'd I put it again?" She swore for the umpteenth time to stop hiding things in places so safe that even she couldn't find them. She certainly couldn't take this risk with the book.

She was all alone as she pushed the book ladder up against an unexamined wall of texts and climbed up; the ceiling was fifteen feet high, and for a moment, Jackie felt dizzy as she surveyed the room from her new vantage point. *Whoa*, she thought. *Slow down.* As she suddenly sat on the top rung, Jon's situation flashed through her mind.

Driving them to her aunt's house, Jon had received an urgent text message. "Here"—he handed his cell phone to Jackie—"read it for me, okay? It's probably Petey."

He was right. Their mother had slipped into a coma, and Jon had to get to the hospital—fast.

Jackie relayed the text as calmly as she could, but she was roiling with emotion that threatened to overcome her. Jon listened stonily, eyes on the road. Only his white-knuckled grip on the steering wheel betrayed his anguish. It was almost too much to bear.

Outside, the New England landscape was bleak and uninviting, a harbinger of the long and difficult winter ahead. The pair had sped through the small town without incident, and Jon quickly pulled up to Shangri-La's grand front entrance. He got out of the car and walked her to the door. "Don't do anything stupid," he warned her. He reached for her hand, and squeezed it tight.

"Who, me?" she said lightly, squeezing back. "You know I live for … for action and adventure …" Her voice trailed off. She couldn't fully confront what she was about to do, and she didn't want to burden Jon with her doubt.

"So,"—she forced a chuckle—"I'm just going to travel back in time, rescue my mother from some voodoo warrior person, and then we'll all come home! Like we were going on a …" She stopped again.

"Long trip?" Jon had said quietly. His hands were shoved deep in his jean pockets, and he was hunched against the cold. Jackie looked up at him, torn.

"I'll be fine." She gave him a little shove and pushed open the front door, which was almost always unlocked. "We'll both be fine." She corrected herself. "We'll all be fine." Then she had marched into the house without looking back.

Now here she was, frantically trying to remember where she'd shoved the book before they raced off to the hospital the night before.

She'd felt its pull for a few weeks now. Late one evening, when she had been curled up in a plush velvet wing chair, book in hand, Wolfe at her feet, she sensed strange vibrations coming from the top shelf of the library. She rubbed her eyes and stretched, shaking her head at one of Jon's Stephen King novels in her lap. She was too scared to read the book in bed, so since it was a Friday night, she decided to stay up reading in the library instead. All the floor and table lamps were on.

"Stop freaking out," she muttered, and willed herself back to *The Shining*. The vibrations continued, this time with a new urgency. Jackie had stood up, choking back her panic. Wolfe got up off the fading Persian rug and whined uneasily.

"Right," she said out loud. "This is getting to be a teeny bit stupid." She glanced out the window. It was a dark night; the moon was clouded over. She half expected to see "redrum" splattered across the French doors. She marched over to the sound, pulsing now from the uppermost bookshelf.

Jackie took a deep breath and swung the book ladder over. She climbed up, and there it was—the magical book, its swirling patterns aglow in a way she'd never seen before. She reached out to touch it—hot.

"No," she'd said to the book. "They said they'd come back for me." She was referring to her parents. "Dad promised." She thought then about the letter her father had written, warning her to return to present time. He and her mother had to track down a criminal on their own, before it was too late. It was too dangerous for Jackie to follow.

So when the book beckoned several weeks ago, Jackie had backed off and stomped into her room, furious now. Where were her parents? Why couldn't she follow them? She was so sick of being a 'good' girl in school, when all she wanted was her parents back.

But now Jackie had no choice. She knew her mother's life was literally at stake. She suddenly remembered where she had stashed the book, and turned to climb down the book ladder.

"Does your aunt Isobel know that you're here?" a shocked voice cut into Jackie's thoughts. She looked down and gasped. Jackie hadn't even noticed Dona Marta, who was plumping pillows on one of the library's large, cushy sofas. Then she slipped off the book ladder and landed gracelessly on the polished parquet floor. She grabbed the book from the lower shelf where she had put it before leaving for the hospital, but it tumbled out of her hands.

The book lay between them. It was open to a page Jackie hadn't seen before.

"*Nossa Senhora*!" Dona Marta invoked the Virgin Mary. Her hands flew to her mouth in an unconscious attempt to cover her shock. Jackie suddenly felt ashamed of herself for cutting school and rummaging through Aunt Isobel's library—a veritable room of treasures. And she was letting Dona Marta down, she who fussed over Jackie as if she were her own child.

Outside, the world gleamed with a brilliance poignant and rare in late autumn, as if to prove the world's warmth one more time before the dark New England winter set in. Long shafts of sunlight flooded through the dull windows and French doors of Aunt Isobel's library; the faded Persian rug seemed to come alive in the remarkable light. The parquet floors shone with an unnatural luster, and the whole room seemed to glow.

Like the book on the floor.

Jackie wrenched her eyes away from the old book and brought her gaze to bear on Dona Marta's expression, anticipating anger, hurt, and disappointment. There was no way to explain to the loyal housekeeper what was happening—or what was about to happen.

But where Jackie expected to see upset and confusion, she saw understanding and concern. Dona Marta's eyes shone with encouragement and determination.

"You must go to your mother," she said. "And you must stop that angry young man," she added.

Jackie started. How did Dona Marta know about her father's former graduate student? With contempt, she thought of the thin man who had a seemingly insatiable appetite for power and control.

Devon. Now there was a real sneak—and a thief. He had never been much of a student, but one late-winter lecture by Professor David Tempo had piqued his interest. It was about time travel. Why was a history professor discussing time travel in a medieval Islamic History course? He had said something about the myths and fantasies Europeans had of the Islamic world during those times; it was these myths that gave rise to the image of the "mysterious Orient," and riches that eluded Europeans even as the Middle Ages drew to a close.

"For instance, take the story of Prester John." The professor strode across a small auditorium stage, hands clasped behind his back, corduroy jacket fraying slightly at the cuffs. He was a charismatic and handsome man, and though he had a loyal female following, Professor Tempo was clearly devoted to his wife, a historian in the Chinese Studies department. Most days, they could be found in the graduate library on campus, deep in discussion of the latest book they were co-authoring.

"Now Prester John was very real to so many Europeans. The story of an avowed Christian somehow caught behind Muslim lines fired the people's imagination in those days. For what did it mean to be a true Christian? To hold fast to one's faith, and to build a kingdom devoted to the glory of God. So many European Christians set off in search of this Prester John

… but to no avail. Did he exist, after all? What purpose would such a story serve?"

A lone hand shot up. Devon rolled his eyes—this girl was always asking questions and drawing Tempo's lectures out. He wished the dumb blonde would shut up, so they could all get out of here.

"Laura?" The professor took a seat on a tall stool on the otherwise bare stage; it was his only prop. He peered down at the young woman.

"Well, for one, wouldn't it serve to boost morale, as proof that Christians could, in fact, withstand the Islamic onslaught? Isn't it true that at this time Spain had already fallen to the Moors?"

"Indeed." The professor nodded thoughtfully.

"But where did such a fantastic story come from?" the girl started. "I mean, it doesn't really sound plausible, and there are no accurate historical records to back it up. At least, not according to our text."

Devon gritted his teeth. If it was one thing he hated, it was a brown-noser—and this girl was one of the worst.

"I have another question," she continued. Devon dug his nails into the auditorium chair. Foam leaked out.

"Go on," Professor Tempo said, nodding. He started to gather up his papers.

"We know of all the great works the Moslems preserved during this time, Greco-Roman pieces and so on, but you once mentioned a set of three books from Samarkand that had the power to transport their readers back in time. Packed in a crate, I think you said, and bound for Baghdad. And when the crate was opened, all sorts of things started happening—like people really did disappear, even whole towns, and—"

Quite out of character, Professor Tempo seemed a bit flustered. Devon noticed with some interest that the man paled as the girl chattered on.

"Ah, yes, that was once a theory of mine, which, to my regret, has since been disproved. Case closed." He glanced at his wristwatch and stuffed his lecture notes into a battered leather briefcase.

For once, Devon was truly interested in the subject. Now—how on earth could he get his hands on those books?

"But, indeed, Laura, here you have another "Prester John"-like story. And consider—when is a myth more relevant than the real story? Why do we hold fast to the stuff of legend?" He jogged down the auditorium steps.

"But since when is time travel not real?" Devon called out. He couldn't help himself.

Professor Tempo stopped in his tracks and stared.

Devon continued, "I mean, why is it that events seem to change as time goes on—and more information is 'discovered'? How do we know that those artifacts weren't plants of some sort—and now the world is able to handle them and all they represent?"

Professor Tempo nodded. "Indeed, what parts of the story are we missing as we sift through time? Whose ideas have we not heard? Where have we *not* looked for clues of the past?" Then he hurried off.

Devon became a man on a mission—he wanted to find those books. With his knowledge and abilities, if he could travel back in time, he could, in fact, rule the world. So he started to apply himself to his studies, and set about researching the story of the mysterious books from Samarkand. Eventually, he enrolled in graduate school, with the specific intent of working with Professor Tempo. The man knew far more than he had revealed, Devon was sure of that. And his certainty increased as Tempo tried to steer him off the topic again and again for his graduate thesis.

Then one night at a graduate student dinner party at the Tempos, Devon stumbled upon one of the famous books. Hidden in plain sight! He knew that the Tempos' unease masked this dark secret. And so it was that Devon had made off with one of the three mysterious books from medieval Samarkand. He had unlocked the power of the books, which could transport a willing reader back in time. As such, he was wandering in the past; the Tempos, with another of the books, were trying to bring him back.

Aunt Isobel owned the third, which now lay now on the library floor. "You must take the book," Dona Marta said. "It is calling you." And she gestured at the glowing page to which the book had opened, a vivid map of colonial Brazil. Amazingly enough, it had landed flat and undamaged, its worn velvet binding intact. The book had no title, Jackie knew, but contained countless secrets of the past. It could bring them back together, and into present time. It could save her mother from an imminent death.

Jackie started: she could see a short red line making its way from the eastern coast to the interior. She took a deep breath; it was now or never. She lunged for the book, red curls flying, and scrambled to her feet. The book pulsed in her hands like a live thing. But she had stood up too fast, and was dizzy. She saw bright spots and instinctively knew she had to breathe deeply to regain her balance. She stared into nothingness, and her vision cleared as she locked eyes with Dona Marta.

And then came the screams, the most horrifying, piteous cries of anguish.

Jackie crumpled to the floor.

BETWEEN WORLDS; TIME UNKNOWN

She reached out and touched something solid. It seemed to her that she felt Dona Marta's fingers, but then she slipped away, hurtling into space. The cries around her intensified, and she was in a stifling, cramped space; it was dark and humid, and she could barely breathe for the stench. She heard a low curse, and then a gurgle. In the darkness, she could make out many, many forms trapped in the dark, crammed together, bound by chains.

Now she locked eyes with a wretched soul; his worn, dull eyes flickered for an instant, as if in recognition. He was lying next to her, arms by his side, drenched in a clammy sweat. The groans intensified around her and she couldn't breathe. *This time I'm really going to die,* she thought. Jackie tried to move, but discovered to her horror, that she was bound like all the other miserable human cargo in the ship's hold.

She was aboard a slave ship.

Some actions are even baser than the people who commit them.
—Jose Maria Machado de Assis

CHAPTER IX:

VOICES FROM HELL

SLAVE SHIP, COAST OF BRAZIL, 1783

As Jackie's eyes adjusted to her hellish surroundings, she was overcome by the beastly conditions of the slave ship. As far as she could make out—and it wasn't very far, actually, because she couldn't see much from her constrained vantage point—she saw bodies, and parts of bodies. She tried to stretch, but succeeded only in butting heads with another captive.

The squalor was inconceivable, and Jackie was plunged into a deep depression at the horror of this ship. Sure, she had read about the trans-Atlantic slave ships, and had seen appalling sketches of how the unfortunates were crammed into the nether parts of the vessel, every possible space taken up by bodies. But she never imagined this: the smell of death and despair, of rot and decay; the utter helplessness of the captives; the moans of those who were beyond pain, past all caring, willing themselves into another world.

Which was what she wanted to do now. *Maybe I'll just die …* She closed her eyes, drowsy from the oppressive heat of the ship's hold. She seemed to be drifting in and out of the voices, and of her own pain, and she lost all sense of self.

"Ow!" Jackie flinched at the searing pain in her back. She felt as if she were being branded by a white-hot poker. "What the—" The heat receded, and Jackie could feel her book digging into her back; it seemed bound about her waist in an awkward fashion.

Then she remembered; the book would become hot to touch when she needed to take specific action. This jab of heat was a reminder, but nothing more, and the book quickly grew cold. It was sending her no clues now; indeed, it was as lifeless and inert as much of Jackie's company in the ship. At any rate, there was no way for Jackie, bound as she was, to pull it out to read. Still, Jackie knew that, somehow, she had to find a way out of this hell, and the book was the only way. If only she knew how.

She stared straight up at the wide planks above her head, desperately trying to will herself out of the slave ship's hold. How had she come to rest here? Then she felt ashamed; though it seemed like an eternity, she knew she'd been in the hold for only a few minutes. Then she thought of the people around her—how long had they been trapped here? She was suddenly seized by a new fear. How long would she be aboard? What if they were just beginning to make the voyage across the Atlantic? Jackie quailed at the thought.

"How did I get here, of all places?" Her voice was little more than a moan.

"The same as the rest of us," a thin voice responded to her left. "Some of us were traded as prisoners of war and marched from the African interior for days on end. And me? The slavers stole me when I was collecting firewood on my own, with no one to hear my muffled screams as they put me in a bag and took me away. I survived the long march to Elmina, the city for which that fort of hell, Elmina Castle, is named."

"And then," another voice continued, "many of us waited in shackles, with none of our kinsfolk, for what would be the next part of this awful journey, alone, yet crowded in with others who had also been torn away from their families. We waited until a ship had been sighted by the Dutch who control Elmina. As the ship grew on the horizon and I knew that my life would be over, I felt worse than dead."

"Because at least death is not this," said a young woman deep in the hold. The ship swayed, and Jackie fought the urge to vomit; if she threw up, she would be lying in it.

"No, death is where our ancestors would come to greet us, smiling, and welcome us to the other side. Here we are nothing …" A great collective wail and chorus rose from the hold, and it seemed to Jackie that the ship could not contain any more misery than it already carried.

Then the ship gave a violent shudder. Mercifully, Jackie passed out. Her last thought as she spiraled into darkness was of gratitude; she couldn't endure much more of this. She'd rather be dead. But what was yet to come was much, much worse.

Some time later, Jackie was yanked out of the ship's hold by her hair. She was numbed beyond all caring, and stumbled as she tripped up into the sunlight. The rough-looking sailor who dragged her out was shocked to see her pale face.

"Oy!" he called out in surprise that was tinged with fear. "A lass!" Who was this wraith? How had she survived the grueling journey from the coast of Angola all the way to Brazil?

"This ship is cursed!" he shouted, releasing her on deck. Several sailors came over to inspect the wan redhead. Jackie leaned over, retching; the fresh air made her dizzy. She carried with her the stench of death. The man who laid hands on her crossed himself several times.

"Like it'll do you any good, João," one of his mates muttered under his breath. A nervous-looking group had assembled around Jackie, who was just now beginning to accept that she was on a slaving ship.

"Yeah, how many of these runs have you made, João?" A young sailor with a British accent smiled grimly. "How many innocents have you sent to their death? How many sailors—like myself—have you pressed into service to handle the 'cargo'?" He spat on the deck, arms folded, and seemed to brace himself for a blow. "And you're crossing yourself for fear of Our Lord. How very

Christian of you, especially since you're in the business of selling humans, God help you!"

"Shut up, English!" Some of the Portuguese crew pushed the teen out of the way. In spite of his tattered clothes, he had an aristocratic bearing, Jackie noticed. She caught his eye. Red-faced, he looked away.

Jackie straightened up, and her surroundings came into focus. She could see that the ship was anchored several hundred feet from a lush coastline that enveloped a busy port. While theirs was the largest anchored vessel, the waters were dotted with many smaller boats as fishermen put out to sea for a day's work. To her left, she saw a small group of men push one such vessel off the beach and into the water by rolling the boat over logs.

"Get into the *jangada*!" a weathered fisherman yelled at his son, who jumped on the small sailboat. Those left behind gave a small wave and returned to their work of repairing fishing nets and cleaning their boats. A young mother stayed for a minute, keeping a watchful eye on her husband and son as they disappeared, off for a day's catch. She clasped a nursing infant tighter to her bosom, and then slowly made her way up the beach.

Was this Brazil? Jackie wondered. The ship had made the perilous journey across the Atlantic, but surely more than a third of the human cargo had perished below deck along the way. Harsh sunlight glinted off the turquoise waters of the harbor and dazzled Jackie. She wondered at such scenes of tranquility amid the horror of the slave ship that had borne her—and hundreds of others—into these calm waters. *Doesn't anyone see us?* she thought, and felt ashamed at her wretched condition. No one saw. No one cared.

Just then, the ship gave a powerful groan, and she was startled out of her reverie. A gangplank was lowered and Jackie noticed up on the far corner of the deck a batch of Africans, chained together. While most of them flinched as buckets of salt water were tossed over them, a few remained motionless.

"Clean 'em up!" came the cry. "Doctor's here!" Striding aboard the ship was one of the slightest, palest men Jackie had ever seen. He was sweating profusely in the humidity of the early morning. The man drew himself up to his full five feet and presented himself to the ship's captain.

"Dr. James Morgan, at your service."

The swarthy captain, a barrel-chested beast of a man whose coat had popped a few buttons, peered down through his shaggy dark eyebrows and stroked his matted beard, which looked as vile as the man it adorned. Jackie hadn't noticed him before. This was surprising, given his fearful appearance, but then, her awareness had been quite clouded by the misery of her experience aboard the slaver.

"I don't know you," the captain said. His unearthly voice, rough as gravel, made Jackie quake. *Like a voice from hell*, she thought.

The little man persisted, oblivious to the very real physical threat the captain posed. "Oh yes, you do," he said. "Here." And he drew a letter out of his coat pocket.

"What d'ye have there?" The captain snatched it out of his hands. He fumbled with the document, dropped it, and snatched it up before it hit the deck. Then he cleared his throat, rustled the paper, and held it taut in his hands. He squinted at the lettering. Jackie was surprised at his discomfort.

The doctor coughed politely. "It should say that we are welcome—"

"Silence!" the captain roared. An awkward quiet hung for a few moments as those on deck held their breath. "All right, then, what d'ye want?"

"It says so right here." The pale doctor pointed to the royal insignia at the bottom of the letter. "I am the chief inspector of all of His Majesty's ships, and that includes, most especially, those who are transported here to help enrich the kingdom's wealth." He seemed so small before the captain, but not the least bit afraid. He drew a deep breath. *To seem taller?* Still hazy from her time below deck, Jackie was confused by her own line of thought. *Who's playing whom here?* she wondered.

"In addition," the doctor continued, "you know the rules of quarantine. We'll not have any plague transported to these shores; since I have survived the plague"—at that a number of crewmen took an involuntary step backward—"I am the local expert on the disease. If your cargo passes muster, you are free to deliver the goods."

"Very well," the captain agreed reluctantly, "but be quick about it, then." He stepped in front of Jackie, but the doctor could see that the slaving captain was hiding something—someone.

"What's this, then?" the doctor cried out. "A white maiden?"

The captain pushed Jackie back. "Aye, and she's none of yer business, so help ye God!"

"Are you mad, then?" the doctor shouted. The captain bared his teeth. This was a disturbing sight, indeed, since most of them were missing. His large, hairy hand went to the hilt of his sword. The entire deck was still, from the captives to the sailors.

"Have you stooped to transporting European girls, my criminal friend?" Jackie saw that the doctor was flushed to the roots of his scalp. He was clearly quite angry. The little man gave a quick signal, and for the first time, Jackie noticed the well-dressed guards behind him.

"Take him into custody," the doctor barked. Two of his muscular young men stepped up, ready for action.

The captain gave a low growl. "I think not!" He motioned for his own men to back him up.

Jackie flinched.

No one moved.

"What the—" the captain roared at his straggly crew. "Are ye forgetting the riches ahead for us!" He stared at the dirty sailors. "We've brought a healthy lot of Africans over, and they're sure to fetch the highest prices! Are ye all mad, ye wastrels?"

Then João, the sailor who had pulled Jackie out on deck, shook himself into action and drew his sword. A few others did the same. "I stand by my captain—as should you all!" he yelled at the crew.

The rest of the crew hung back, mutinous. Most of them had borne the brunt of the captain's ill temper throughout the long crossing. He didn't want to leave marks on the slaves, so his anger was often vented on those he wouldn't be selling at slave market. Jackie noticed that many of the crew were fairly young. Then "English," the teenage boy, spoke up.

"Why should we?" he spat. "Most of us were pressed into service—and aboard a slaving ship at that!" He gave a violent shudder as he glanced over to the uncomprehending Africans. "'Tis against God's will to enslave others!"

"God's will?" João pulled his fist back. "The Bible speaks of slavery, fool! God wills that Christians rule over savages!"

The doctor had had enough. He gave a slight nod to his own men, who had come aboard amidst the hubbub without permission. "Now," he said quietly.

At that, his guards sprang into action. They drew their pistols and surrounded the captain and his loyalists. A dozen more clambered over the side of the boat, swords drawn menacingly.

"What the—" the captain sputtered in shock. A husky young guard cuffed him on the back of the head. The captain turned to respond but was halted by the sight of the seven-foot soldier. The guard grinned.

"That's right," the doctor said in a voice reserved for soothing colicky babies. "Have a seat."

The prisoners were knocked to their knees, and their legs were kicked out. Now the African captives looked on in interest, and some even started smiling at the sight of their tormentors being bound together as they once were.

"Where is the harbor master?" the captain roared. "He'll have yer head for this! I have valuable property aboard! This is a special shipment, I tell ye! And—" He was finally silenced by the large young guard, who clocked him on the head. The captain crumpled to the deck like a rag doll. The guard looked guiltily at the mild-mannered doctor. "Sorry, sir."

"No need to be sorry, lad, when it comes to silencing one of God's abominations—slavers!" The doctor made another quick motion, and some other guards rushed to unshackle the slaves.

"Careful, now, they'll be skittish," warned the doctor. Indeed, some of the captives had backed away in fear; others held out their bound hands to be freed.

"Oy—look out!" cried a sailor. One of the Africans rushed to the railing, and made to throw himself overboard. It was the young man who had been chained beside Jackie in the wretched hold.

"No!" Jackie raced to him. "You're safe now, trust me!" Her aunt's book warmed her back, and she knew it was giving her the power to speak the dialect she needed. The miserable teen with dark, sunken cheeks climbed down and took her outstretched hands.

"Miss." He came up beside her, his eyes curious. "It was you who were with us down below."

She nodded. "I know. It's hard to explain. But it seems that everything will turn out all right." A small group of slaves crowded around her, touching her long red hair and murmuring in wonder.

Jackie looked around and smiled at the doctor, who stared at her, open-mouthed. Hope surged inside her. She was going to live, after all. She held fast to her new African friend.

The captain and his slavers were bound and gagged, and were pushed below deck even as the rest of the slaves were being brought up to their freedom. The English teen helped out, cheeks flushed with excitement. He was in the hands of a very different sort of captain for now—one he'd serve willingly, and in good conscience.

Then Jackie cast her eyes out across the harbor. Though the ship was anchored well away from the shore, she could hear shouts of confusion from the port, as well-dressed gentlemen strained to see what had happened aboard the ship. She squinted, trying to make sense of the scene. Behind them were carriages with liveried African slaves holding their horses' reins. She could make out a few white ladies in calico dresses, with black women hovering by their sides, fanning them in the heat. Farther back from the port, away from the narrow cobblestone streets, rose a large baroque church, surrounded by whitewashed two-story buildings with brightly colored wooden shutters. Jackie saw that someone had clambered to the bell tower of the ornate church, the tallest building in town, and begun to pull on a rope.

And so the alarm was raised: a slaving ship had been overtaken! The shouts rose in urgency, and the ladies in their carriages strained forward. A few men jumped into rowboats, guns in hand. A cannon fired from a whitewashed fort. Jackie hadn't noticed the weapons before. The commotion on the dock grew to a frenzy.

"That's it, then," the doctor said, grinning. "Time to set sail." He gave a shout: "Anchors away!" Then the little man gave a chuckle, and patted Jackie's arm.

"Welcome to Brazil."

I deny that villainy is ever necessary.
It is impossible that it should ever be necessary
for any reasonable creature to violate all the laws of justice, mercy,
and truth.
—John Wesley

CHAPTER X:

THE PRICE OF FREEDOM

Later, much later, when the ship was making steady progress north, the doctor invited Jackie to dine with him.

"Glad to see you restored to your natural beauty, m'dear," he said gently. Then he gave a broad smile. When they had anchored briefly to take on provisions, Jackie had managed to wash up in one of the island's many streams. While she was awed by the natural beauty of the island, she made quick work of it, as she realized that time was of essence. The locals were hard on their heels, she knew, and they were pressing to reach a safe destination. *Like a maritime version of the Underground Railroad,* she'd mused, washing herself in the crystal clear water. But she hadn't been sure. The new captain—the ship's doctor—had not revealed the full extent of his plans. All they knew was that they were heading to a safer place, where the Africans would be set free. Jackie wasn't sure what would happen to the former captain and his loyalists, but she decided to wait and see; the doctor seemed like a good man.

"Now then," said the doctor. He sat her down in the captain's quarters, which he had thoroughly cleaned out to rid all traces of the barbaric occupant before him. He handed Jackie a steaming cup of coffee. She took care to smooth the front of her long calico dress and tried not to think of how they'd come by such a refined garment aboard the slaving ship. Still, it fit her perfectly.

She gave an involuntary shudder, and the doctor looked at her in concern, but was too discreet to inquire. Instead, he asked, "Where are you really from, dear child?"

Jackie's eyes filled with tears at his kind tone. She set her cup down on a nearby tray, hand shaking.

The doctor noted her distress and changed the subject. "You might well wonder the same of me!" He gave a short laugh and tugged at his waistcoat. In spite of the events of the last few hours, he remained perfectly groomed. "I have a daughter your own age, and she is ever hounding me with questions."

"Like what?" Jackie inquired in a small voice.

"Oh, where am I going? What is my mission? Why do some journeys take longer than others? When will I come home?" The doctor frowned slightly.

"And where is home to you, sir?" Jackie asked.

"Why, England, of course," the doctor responded with a hint of pride.

"'Of course'?"

"Yes—England is home to the abolitionist movement." The doctor sat up a bit straighter. "We're small in number, but the movement is growing. Even now, our ships are intercepting slavers, and turning them back to the coast of Africa."

"But what about this ship? We're already in Brazil!" Jackie blurted out.

The doctor was grim. "Yes, this is true. Most of the slavers end up here."

Jackie smoothed her skirt once more, but her brow was knitted in confusion.

"You see," the doctor explained, "most of the Africans who are unfortunate enough to, ah, participate in this trade are sent here to plant and reap sugar." He sighed. "It is a deadly crop, in more ways than one can fathom."

Jackie nodded. She had learned that the slaves on sugar plantations were worked virtually to death—this was particularly true in the French colony of St. Domingue—and as such, were not "reproducing themselves," as Ms. Thompson had delicately put it. So there was a ceaseless demand for fresh slaves from Western Africa during this time.

She thought about the captain and his loyal men, and drew her brows together. They were clearly of African descent—what were they doing in this brutish business? She asked the doctor about it.

"Wouldn't someone like the captain want to join the antislavery cause?"

"Like the captain?" The doctor echoed, arching a thick white brow. "Surely you don't mean the color of his skin?"

Jackie blushed, feeling quite awkward. "Yes," she mumbled.

Dr. Morgan nodded. "I see," he said, and cleared his throat. "Well, in the first place, the captain is Brazilian—and here, anyone with any European blood isn't considered truly African, or even black, at all."

"So racism isn't an issue, then?" Jackie was surprised.

"Racism? Oh, do you mean whether their race affects the way people are treated? No, but not quite the problem as is the case farther north, in England's former colonies, now the so-called 'United States'." The British doctor squinted, thinking how best to explain himself. Then he walked over to his cabin door, which stood open.

"See there, our unfortunate captain?" He pointed to the very unhappy dark man, now tied to his former crew. They had just been let out on deck for some fresh air, with the English teen keeping a watchful eye on them. "He is a mulatto. Most likely his mother was a slave, and his father was white. Then there's João"—he picked out another prisoner—"now he is probably a *caboclo*, a type of *mestiço*, of a white father and Indian mother. You are probably more familiar with the word *mestizo*." He tapped his chin thoughtfully. "And I'm not sure if there are any *cafuzos* aboard—"

"*Cafuzos?*" Jackie broke in.

"Oh, that's someone with African and Indian heritage. The point is," the doctor continued, "in Brazil, while there are many racial classifications, anyone with European blood is considered 'whiter' than one without. There are Africans, who are brought here as slaves, and then—there's the rest of Brazilian society, most of which is of mixed descent."

A loud crack of thunder interrupted his discourse. Jackie jumped at the terrifying sound.

"Just an afternoon, shower, nothing to worry about," Dr. Morgan reassured her. He helped himself to another cup of coffee, in spite of the midafternoon heat. He glanced out his cabin window; in another hour or so, he knew, great thunderclouds would roll in. The ensuing downpour would do little to dissipate the heat, but at least it would clear away some of the humidity. He mopped his face with a linen handkerchief and smiled at the bright, earnest redhead seated across from him. Jackie really did remind him of his daughter, Elsa, who was inquisitive, thoughtful, and bursting with ideas. He had been right to school her in rhetoric and in the classics; it gave him much joy to converse with an intelligent young lady. "Yes, lass, now what is it?"

Jackie masked her fear with another question. "This might be simpler to answer: why are we drinking coffee?" Jackie pointed to her porcelain cup. "I thought the British only ever drank tea."

The doctor laughed. "Right you are, but my mother was an Italian, and she swore by the healing properties of the coffee bean. Clears the intestines, you know." He coughed; perhaps he shouldn't have been so indelicate. "This coffee"—he peered into the murky liquid—"is the finest available. The planters of São Paulo are blessed with perfect soil and climate conditions."

"And an abundance of slave labor," Jackie volunteered.

"Indeed." Dr. Morgan set his cup down. "The planters think that it makes better economic sense for them to use 'free' and 'expendable' labor. Thus they refuse to give up slaving. They believe that if they have to pay their workers, they'd have to give up much in the way of profit. But they are wrong. Slavery makes no economic sense at all."

Jackie was confused. "But aren't profits higher if labor is free?"

"Ah." The doctor leaned back and folded his hands over his small belly. "But to say that slave labor is free labor is completely false. And so what the Paulistas— those from São Paulo—believe to be true will actually bring about great economic ruin for them in the end."

"Because you'll chase down slaving ships and cause them to lose money?" Jackie asked.

"No." Her rescuer shook his head and replenished his coffee. Dr. Morgan paused for a moment, admiring the delicate pattern on the porcelain. "Because slave labor is actually quite unproductive." He looked at Jackie. "Would you work harder if you were forced to do so, or if you were willing?"

"Well, I'd certainly work hard if I were scared for my life," she answered. She couldn't see where he was going, but she suddenly thought of her mother. Now that was a scary situation. "If someone threatened me or my family with violence, of course I'd work hard to avoid that fate." Jackie pushed a stray red lock behind her ear.

"But would you be more productive if you were afraid, or if you were willing? Which would yield better results?"

"I guess ... if I were willing," Jackie answered slowly. "I'm more motivated when I'm not afraid."

For some strange reason, all she could think about was her best 1500-meter track experience. Her coach had thrown her into that race instead of the 3000 meters because another runner was injured. Coach had told her to "go out and have fun." She had no pressure on her at all, as she was not known for her speed in this event. She was loose and fluid the whole way though, and until the bell lap had felt pretty comfortable, and she had come in first. While running track was a far cry from forced labor, she thought she understood.

"Well," she began slowly, "didn't Adam Smith write about the importance of self-interest and its connection to economic production? How it was a good thing—something like that?"

Dr. Morgan laughed in sheer delight. "You are full of surprises, my dear! That you are familiar with Smith's writings is most impressive! Still," he continued, "you are correct. And therein lies the economic argument against slavery. When labor is unwilling, it is unproductive. The pace of work is slower than it should be. And in addition, there is less demand for advances that could speed up productivity, and so an economy remains rooted in backwardness. For instance—"

Just then, they were interrupted by a shout. "We've arrived, sir!"

The two of them walked out onto the deck, arm in arm. The ship had anchored in a sheltered cove. Jackie drew her breath; the water was perfectly clear, and she could see all the way to the sandy ocean floor. Lush green vegetation surrounded a perfectly white beach that glistened in the late morning sun. They had arrived— but where?

Jackie felt safe with the paternal doctor and was not quite willing to move into uncharted territory alone. But she knew that her mother was deep in the Brazilian jungle, and she had to get off this ship to find her.

On shore, a tall, noble African stepped out of the bush. Jackie gasped at his regal bearing, and a cry went up from the captives aboard the ship. Some tried to clamber over the side. Arms were outstretched in greeting; the doctor's men made haste to lower a boat to bring the would-be slaves to shore. As Jackie watched the first boat row to the beach, Dr. Morgan explained that the ship would unload all the former prisoners, and they would be escorted to safety.

"How can they be safe here?" Jackie asked. "Aren't we still in Brazil?"

The good doctor smiled. "Yes indeed," he replied. "But it is in the interior—away from the coasts—that the runaways live in free communities."

"How is that possible?" Jackie asked. Another small boat made its way to the beach. "How can they be free in a slaving nation?"

"Look, my dear. " The doctor waved his arm at the lush expanse just beyond the coastline. "Tell me what you see."

Jackie was confused. This was like being back in class, and she felt frustrated, as she sometimes did in school, that he wasn't just giving her the answer.

"I see … green, green, and still more green." She was beginning to feel annoyed. Sweat trickled down her back.

"Indeed you do." The doctor squinted at the dense vegetation, as if he were trying to see more. "And isn't that a nice hiding place?" Jackie nodded, her interest piqued once more, as he explained that Brazil's lush vegetation provided more than ample cover for runaways.

"Here in Brazil, and also in parts of the Caribbean, there are many, many runaway slave communities. In parts of the Caribbean, they are called *marrons,* because that is the Spanish word for highlands, where they flee. In Brazil, the safe havens are called *quilombos.*"

Jackie shook her head. "I had no idea," she said softly.

"Of course you didn't," the doctor looked at her sharply. *What a strange girl,* he thought. Then he continued, glad of a receptive audience. "The largest of these *quilombos* was Palmares, which held, it is rumored, up to twenty thousand runaways at one time. No one knows for certain. Certainly no white person would know. At any rate, that is where they are headed now—to a *quilombo* where they may live in freedom."

Jackie was stunned—and thrilled. "That's amazing." She watched the former captives, still hesitant, but markedly relieved, being led off into the jungle. The English teen who had been pressed into service aboard the ship encouraged the Africans as they made their way ashore.

"What will happen to him—and the others who were pressed into service aboard the slaver?" Jackie pointed to the tall blond youth. He was joking in sign language with the Africans who were waiting aboard the ship.

"I will offer them service with me; my group is the last line of defense off the coast of Brazil," said Dr. Morgan. "If the English navy fails to intercept the slavers in the Atlantic, then we are the final hope for the unfortunate souls who are shipped from Africa."

"But doesn't the English navy press sailors into involuntary service as well?" Jackie clapped a hand over her mouth. She didn't want to be rude to her rescuer. Still, she had read that much of the navy at this time was no more than conscripted labor. It didn't seem much different from slavery to her.

"Yes, that is an unfortunate practice that continues under questionable captainship; it is frowned upon, as it breeds mutiny in the ranks. However, that is not the case here. The boy and his friends will be free to go as they like. God willing, they will lead more fortunate lives from here on out."

And what about me? Jackie wondered. A slight breeze rifled her hair and dried the sweat that had collected in the small of her back. For the life of her, she could not fathom how eighteenth-century women tolerated long, full-sleeved dresses in the semitropical heat.

The last group of Africans was getting ready to board a rowboat. Jackie was at a loss as to her own situation. She turned away from the rail and looked up at one of the tall masts. It seemed to reach into the dazzling azure sky, all but disappearing into the bright afternoon light.

And then came her sign. Aunt Isobel's book, now bound tightly to her upper right thigh, well out of sight underneath her billowing dress, suddenly became quite hot. She grimaced.

"Excuse me," she said stiffly to the doctor, who was by now busy paying attention to the last of the group to leave.

"You have my leave, dear child," the doctor said distractedly. He pulled out a pocket watch and flipped it open with a practiced move. "We haven't much time, lads!" he shouted. "We've got to catch the land breeze and set sail soon!"

Jackie wasn't so sure that she'd be joining them. She backed away and looked for a quiet place to hide. Eventually she made her way to an aft cabin and bolted the door shut. It was small, and in spite of the scouring the ship had received in the last few hours, it still reeked of sweat—and death.

She sat gingerly on a lower bunk and lifted her skirts. "What a pain!" she muttered. She had always hated fussy clothing. The book was burning hot now, and she bit her lip to keep from crying out. She unwrapped the muslin cloth that bound it to her leg.

Then the book fell open to a map of colonial Brazil; it was marked by heavy calligraphy. "Okay," she whispered, "so where am I supposed to go now?" As if on cue, a deep red mark appeared on the eastern coast of Brazil and snaked its way north, veering towards the interior.

"From to Pernambuco … to Alagoas … and then …?" The words felt strange in her mouth as she sounded them out. She grew dizzy, and it seemed that she could hear rhythmic music and a wild stomping of feet. She couldn't identify the instruments. As she stared at the yellowed page, a "J" appeared in what seemed to be jungle. She thought she heard a woman humming a lullaby. It all seemed so familiar.

"J is for … Jackie—and Judith!" She snapped the book shut; it was cooling down by now. Jackie bound the book to her thigh once more, taking care to secure it well.

Her course of action decided, Jackie went over to the captain's desk, dipped his quill pen in ink, and wrote a short note to the good Dr. Morgan.

"Impressive." Though her penmanship was not quite legible, her note certainly looked pretty. She at least wanted to leave him an explanation. Pleased, she shook the pen out—and ink splattered all over her fresh note.

"Agh!" Jackie was frustrated. It looked like a large spider had exploded on the last page of the captain's log. She shuddered at the sight. Never mind all that now. She set the inkwell down on the upper left corner of the page to let her note dry and call attention to her words.

Then she stood up and opened the cabin door. "Coming, Mom."

The one who throws the stone forgets; the one who is hit remembers forever.
—Angolan proverb

CHAPTER XI:

PARADISE DENIED

BRAZILIAN JUNGLE, 1783

The slender man with thinning blond hair stormed his way through the jungle, hacking a path back to the town of Pernambuco with a fury that frightened all living beings out of his way. Even a fist-sized spider, swollen from a sumptuous meal of fresh flies and other insects, scurried up a tree limb at the onslaught of this crazed white man. Normally, the hairy black spider might have protected its territory with a venomous sting that would drop a trespasser in five minutes flat. But not today. The man was moving too fast.

"Curse them all!" Devon snarled, barely pausing to wipe away rivers of sweat that threatened his vision. He was too enraged to fully assess his discomfort, which must have been great indeed. For here in the steamy jungle, the *mato*, everything seemed coated in wet, it was so humid. The haze of the noonday sun filtered down onto a dark jungle floor that seemed alive; all manner of creatures moved languidly about it in a heat-induced trance.

He had been frustrated in his own attempts to find the *quilombos*. He wanted his own kingdom, deep in the Brazilian jungle, and expected to control his subjects through knowledge divined in his ancient book. He had persuaded a group of runaways to follow him deep into the jungle, where he would show them the way to 'heaven on earth.'

Naturally, the runaways were distrustful of the strange white man who had tried to gain their sympathies. But through the use of his magic book, he had discovered a secret path that led them to an offshoot of a large *quilombo*, a path that could only be found with an understanding of West African symbols. The book, however, showed the way, and the runaways recognized the carvings in the trees at once. They would have taken longer to find the secret path without Devon, and they were grateful; it was only a matter of time before the overseer and his men, perhaps even the local militia, would gain on them and drag them back to their lives of toil and deprivation. In a small clearing, one of the former slaves had found a traditional mask, used in rituals of thanks and praise; a small drum was unearthed as well. Of course, the runaways had no way of knowing that Devon had planted these items days earlier.

It was at that instant that a red-haired woman in her late forties had stepped out of the clearing, looking just as surprised as they were.

"Stop!" she shouted. "We can talk!" She moved toward Devon, who was staring at her in shock. It was Judith Tempo. But how—

He recovered quickly. "There! She is your old master's witch! Look at her hair!" Indeed, they were shocked by the ferocity of its color; it was like nothing they had ever seen before. At Devon's urging, they bound the woman, although they were surprised at her strength and agility. The runaways taunted her, dancing around her slight figure as she sagged against a post. They were filled with hate for all of her white race. Devon wisely slipped into the shadows and watched.

Somehow, time in the jungle ceased to have meaning, and he eventually fell asleep, bored by the dancing and singing. He would keep Judith where she was for now; he knew that David, her husband, would have no way of finding her if she had their copy of the secret book. *Now there's a thought.* He smiled to himself. *I should just take the book away from her now, burn it, and the two Tempos would be stranded in eighteenth-century Brazil forever.*

It was at that very moment that a loud thunderclap erupted overhead.

"Look!" One of the group pointed to a wicked shaft of lightening that split in three jagged streaks as it raced to the ground. "The gods must be angry!" The sky darkened, and then opened up. In an instant, hail pelted them. A torrential downpour blinded them as they rushed for cover in the bush.

The fierce storm vanished almost as soon as it began. Devon had been knocked out by a fist-sized piece of hail. When he came to, they were gone—the runaways, Judith—all vanished without a trace.

"A pox on them!" he cursed, furious at being abandoned. He didn't care what became of Judith, but how was he to find the *quilombos*? And after all that he had promised! He flipped open his book. Stone-cold, the pages all but reproached him for his foolishness. Devon pressed his thin lips together and refrained from hurling the book into the jungle.

Now Devon crashed through the sluggish undergrowth in anger, his movements startling sleeping birds up in the highest branches of the jungle trees, where they watched him in curiosity. He was a man alone, with only a strangely marked book to guide him back to safety, a book that was offering him nothing useful at the moment.

Devon thought back on the Angolan prince he'd rescued not too far from one of the local *fazendas*, or plantations. The tall African had run away from a particularly abusive overseer, one who enjoyed breaking his slaves before he set them to work—until they collapsed for good.

Devon had shared coffee with the *mestre*—the overseer—once, when he was first transported to Brazil. The man had a cruel streak as cold and hard as steel, forged from a childhood of deprivation. He had come to Brazil in search of his fortune when he was but nine, having learned that life in Lisbon could offer him nothing more than an impoverished life on the streets; his mother had died in childbirth, and his father, left with five hungry children, drank himself into a stupor each night. One by one, the children left on their own or simply disappeared, until only Jorge was left.

One evening, Jorge's father rolled over on his pallet and vomited onto the dirt floor, as he had every night since his wife had died. The stench seeped into every corner of the windowless room. The man wiped his face with a rag that was stiff as crust; as far as Jorge knew, it had never been washed.

"You're still here?" Jorge's father reached for something to throw at his remaining child—a brick, a shoe, a belt—but the effort wore him out. He collapsed back onto his pallet. Jorge pulled his rags about him more tightly, and remained curled in the corner.

In the morning, his father was dead. Jorge walked out of that room and onto the first ship he could find that would take him as far away from his wretched life in Lisbon. Scarcely had he snuck aboard the ship that Jorge discovered that his previous experience with misery had only been an introduction into a world even more cruel. He spent most of the journey to Brazil in a haze of confusion, pain, and fear. Reduced to an automaton that obeyed commands and submitted to blows, he ceased to exist.

Once on Brazilian shores, however, Jorge wandered off in the confusion of Recife. It was colorful and warm, not grainy and damp as in Lisbon. To his mind, Lisbon would forever be cast in hues of gray. Brazil, however, seemed lush and full of life, and ripe for the picking.

Then Jorge noticed a group of people whose misery was far greater than his own. They were the first Africans he'd ever seen. They were bound together, heads hung low; the women were stripped and jeered at by a jaded crowd. They were for sale, and Jorge was fascinated that a group of adults could be more powerless than he. Then he watched as a strong male African was pulled aside and beaten by a white man half his size. Jorge felt a strange, electric sort of energy coursing through him. He wanted to be that white man. He wanted to inflict pain on others, rather than receive it. And he wanted to be able to take on bigger men—and to prove to himself and the world that he was, in fact, quite powerful.

Thus it was that Jorge came to oversee Tomas da Silva's *engenho*, or plantation, one of the largest in Pernambuco, where his cruel treatment of slaves was legendary. But he never destroyed valuable "property"; oh no. Instead he was able to wring every ounce of strength from his master's slaves and use them until they were too worn out to breathe. He was richly rewarded for handling his master's investments properly, and for increasing production on the growing sugar plantation. His master knew vaguely of Jorge's cruel measures, but he was not interested in the beatings, the brandings, the slicings, the lashings—all of which were administered with a touch that enabled the slave to go on working the next day.

As Devon had listened to the overseer brag over coffee—Jorge never touched alcohol, as it weakened his senses—he was overcome by revulsion. *That's just sick*, Devon had thought. *There has to be another way to grow an empire.* This, after all, was what he sought above all else; since childhood, he had imagined holding court in a large palace, slaves and women ready to indulge his every whim. He saw himself as a noble warrior, though he never thought in great detail about actually *doing* battle. Just winning, and enjoying his ill-gotten bounty.

And he did not like to be played for a fool. Devon had decided that he would be a benevolent ruler of sorts in a remote part of Brazil—and in 1783, the population was very much concentrated in the coastal areas, with the exception of Sao Paulo. He wanted a life of ease, a gentleman's paradise, and had pictured himself swinging in a hammock, sipping refreshing drinks prepared for him by doe-eyed beauties with long, shiny hair. He imagined striding purposefully through the orange groves of his *fazenda*; his workers would be grateful that he was not a tyrant, but rather a benevolent patriarch.

Devon fumed as he continued to chart a rough course through the *mato* toward town. Every now and then, he'd pat his satchel, just to make sure that his book from Samarkand was still there. It was, after all, his only way out, should he need it.

"I'll show them all!" he swore. This time, he was thinking of his own family, the Pearsons, controllers of a vast real-estate empire. If it weren't for his grandfather, he wouldn't have to be here plotting a way to create his own fortune. He could be swinging in that hammock, drink in hand, on one of his grandfather's resort islands—or better yet—on an island his grandfather had bequeathed to him.

But no ... Grandfather had determined that inheritance made a man weak. Made all of them weak. Grandfather was convinced that this would water the stock down, as hangers-on would be attracted to the Pearson family fortune and drag the younger generation down into scandal or drugs.

So while James Michael Pearson controlled several billion dollars worth of real estate from Hawaii to Manhattan and now China, at age seventy he was beginning to divest himself of his vast fortune. Oh, he still liked to play the game—he loved the chase, the hunt, the energy surging through him as he planned his next venture. But these days, he was more excited about giving his money away to worthwhile causes and was pleased that most of his family had joined him in building up the Pearson Foundation. James Michael Pearson, fearsome real estate tycoon and political power broker, wanted to put his money to good.

His grandson Devon was not included in his plans. At all. And thus it was that Devon found himself hunting down get-rich-quick schemes while still a teenager in college. But those schemes always required an inordinate amount of serious work. Except one.

Devon slowed down now and stopped to scoop up a mouthful of water from a swiftly running stream. It was lukewarm. "Ugh." He spat it out. *That was the problem with earlier times*, he thought. *No friggin' vending machines.*

As he sat on a fallen tree and retied his sweaty boots, fear and doubt worried him like an old woman. He had tried to take all precautions. He'd made sure that Judith Tempo was captured and handed over to a group of black magic worshippers. But then in the middle of a crazy dance ceremony, she'd passed out, and a heavy rain had fallen, scattering everyone. When the sky cleared not five minutes later—it was like that in the afternoons here, Devon was discovering—Judith was gone. Worse, so was the Angolan prince who was supposed to help him build his Brazilian empire. In fact, the jungle was silent, and he was all alone.

"You'll be sorry," Devon said to no one in particular. He clenched his jaw and stood, hiking up his pants. "You have no idea." And as he made his way back into town, he determined to find the one person who could help him on his new quest—Jorge. Devon suppressed a shudder of revulsion as he thought of the man's eyes, dark as evil and as forbidding as death.

His mind was made up. His eyes were flat.

"It's party time."

Night was running after itself.
—Jorge Amado

Chapter XII:

The Ghost of Zumbi

Runaway slave community, Brazil, 1783

Judith stepped outside the medicine woman's hut in the predawn darkness and pulled a faded cotton shawl a bit tighter around her thin shoulders. Like most of those who lived in this community, she was barefoot, mindful of her step as she set off with Elva to collect herbs hidden in the deepest part of the jungle. Elva, sure-footed and nimble as she picked her way through the undergrowth, pursued a path that was all but invisible to Judith.

"This is for Marco, who has trouble sleeping." Elva put valerian root in her basket. "One of the few remedies from white people."

Judith nodded; she knew that valerian root was native to Europe. "Why can't he sleep?" she asked, remembering the man's bleak face when he shuffled to Elva for help.

"He is haunted by dreams of his old life on the *engenho*, the slave plantation." Marco was a twenty-three-year-old who had cut sugarcane under a cruel overseer for the last five years. In that time he had seen the woman he loved beaten to death for not working hard enough in the fields when she was pregnant. The child she carried was his, and did not survive its mother's cruel fate. So Marco ran away, fearing nothing, certainly not the loss of his life. He had lost all he ever cared about, anyway. Three months ago he had ended up in this free community.

"The past visits him every night—like a jealous lover," Elva observed. "We must loosen its grip on Marco. This should work." She sifted through her basket. "And this—we'll give him some *guaraná* to stimulate the senses and appetite; perhaps some *arapuana*, for his upset stomach."

Judith squatted beside Elva, wondering at the roots she held in her hand. Beside the little medicine woman, Judith felt large and clumsy—and terribly white, conspicuous against the darker jungle colors. "Where did you learn all this?" she asked. She waved at the basket of *guaraná*, *pau d'arco*, and luscious berries that were poison if consumed alone.

Elva smiled, revealing a gap-toothed grin. "My mother," she said, "and—here." She tapped her head. Judith knew that Elva had extraordinary powers of intuition—how else could she have whisked her away during that awful ceremony with the dancing, howling masks? Elva had sensed her distress.

As Elva reached out to pull a thin root from unyielding soil, she froze in mid-action. Then she clenched her worn brown hand, digging her fingers deep in her palm. Her eyes rolled backward in her head, and she moaned.

"Elva?" Judith reached her hand out to her friend's shoulder. "What is it?"

Far overhead, in a small opening above the dense jungle trees, Judith could see two birds circling each other. They issued unnatural, plaintive cries that pierced the dense foliage and were just as quickly absorbed in the darkness below. Judith had become accustomed to the dimness of this part of the *mato*, but after glancing up at the birds she had to readjust to the hushed world in which she and Elva moved quietly.

At the moment, however, Elva wasn't moving much. Rather, she had sunk to the ground in a fit of shivers. Spittle collected in the corner of her mouth. Then she began to speak.

"The nestling seeks her way, blindly, but surely … homing in on a temporary haven. She has plotted a collision course with destiny, agh … come to the Mother … the Great Goddess …. No, no, can she be falling from the sky …?" Elva crumpled into herself.

Judith's heart beat wildly. "Who are you talking about? Elva, wake up!" She shook the older woman a bit more roughly than she'd intended. Elva didn't move.

Then Judith felt the familiar warmth of the book that was always bound to her side. If Elva wasn't speaking to hear, this book certainly was.

She pulled it out, and the pages fell open to a fading map of colonial Brazil. She frowned at a dark patch in the middle of the ink rendering; since when had the book gotten stained? She had always taken care to protect it from the elements. The stain seemed to have swirling edges that were almost alive, reaching out to unfurl at the edge of the page.

"Jackie!" her mother gasped. The dark patch was a replica of her daughter's profile, spread now across the entire map of Brazil. Her long hair swirled around her as if she were caught in a malevolent maelstrom; there was no way out. But Jackie remained focused and clear, in spite of all that swirled around her.

Then the image faded, and a glowing red mark appeared on the page.

"The *quilombo*," Judith muttered. "Okay, I'm supposed to be here, and we're going back in a bit, but what else?" Then she noticed something odd, which Elva, in her trance-like state, described even as Judith recognized the images amassing on the coastal area directly east of the *quilombo*.

"War … the hunter and the hunted finally meet face to face …"

Judith shuddered. Exactly what she had feared: preparations were being made to directly attack the *quilombo*. This is what she saw in her book: glistening spears and muskets; cannons being set into place; men shouting preparations and horses being saddled for war. Where was David when she needed him?

She had last seen her husband across a muddy street in the bustling town of Recife. He was driving a carriage horse forward and she had to step back so as not to be trampled. In doing so, she had backed directly into

Devon, who had taken her captive in the jungle. She had escaped, thanks to Elva, and now Jackie had joined them in 18th century Brazil! Clearly, they were all pulled here to prevent a terrible disaster, most likely involving Devon.

"Jackie, come home," she whispered. "I'm here."

This was a Tempo tradition, calling home wherever the family was at the time. As traveling professors, the Tempos had long taught their inquisitive daughter that "home" might be a hotel, an inn, university housing— or even a tent. Home was a concept, a feeling; it was portable and indestructible. They carried home with them wherever they went together.

"Please," she whispered, "come to home to Mom."

Deep in the jungle, Jackie froze. She had been making steady progress toward—where? But she knew not to question her instinct. The book was her guide; she was on the right track.

A twig snapped softly somewhere to her left. Jackie ignored it and kept pushing forward, stepping lightly, freer now that she had changed into men's clothing. She had tried to pen an explanation to Dr. Morgan just before she left the ship, swimming ashore after the last of the African captives had been transported to safety and as the ship prepared to continue its journey after dinner. She hoped he wouldn't worry. When she finally made it to the beach, she saw a lone figure on the deck; it was the English boy, who seemed to know much more than he was letting on. He had raised his cap to her in salute. The sky burst into brilliant colors as the sun sank beneath the horizon, and Jackie waved back. Then she started her trek towards her mother, hurrying in the falling darkness.

Much further north, and hundreds of years later, Jon sat by his mother's hospital bed. Petey lay curled up beside her, and the two of them slept, his younger brother careful not to disturb the tubes that hooked their mother up to several IVs. It was late, but Jon didn't feel like leaving—not yet. He stepped into the hallway and pulled out the crumpled document packet that Jackie had thrust at him this afternoon when he took her back to her aunt Isobel's home.

Where was Jackie now? He sighed as he unfolded the packet, and looked for document five, where her mother appeared to be tied to a stake, some sort of voodoo ceremony in process around her.

He frowned, flipping back and forth through the documents, then sighed in relief. It was right where it should have been; he was rushing as usual.

"So impatient," his mother would have chided him—if she were awake.

He squinted at the paper, and sat back in shock. The document had changed.

Jackie's mother was no longer there.

The voodoo ceremony was still detailed in great relief, but in the background, deep among the dense shrubbery, appeared to be the outline of a young girl in men's clothing. Jon rubbed his eyes; it was late, he was seeing things. He looked again.

What he was seeing was Jackie.

BRAZILIAN JUNGLE, 1783

Now she was certain she was being followed, and she picked up the pace, squaring her shoulders and digging in. *Loose,* she urged herself, *get loose.* She flew over ancient roots and whispering streams. She jumped over fallen trees.

Another snap, again to her left. Jackie dared not look, even as she noticed a blur of motion in the brush. *Mom,* she cried out silently. *Dad, Jon, anyone.* Her breath came in ragged spurts as she choked back panic.

The underbrush was getting thicker, slowing her down. Something soft dropped onto her shoulder and she brushed it off—a tarantula the size of her hand scrambled into the bush.

"Oh!" She started clawing through what was very thick jungle now, blinded by fear, sobbing quietly with fright. But still she was driven—or dragged—forward by a force that moved through her and beyond her.

"Am I nothing, then?" she spat out to the living, breathing, waiting wild, flailing at the underbrush. Tears streaked down her grimy face. Why was everything so difficult? She thought back on her horrific journey to Brazil, and of tumbling through time. "Am I not free— at all?" Why was it that her whole life seemed to be about waiting—or running?

Then all at once, a peace filled her whole being with a warmth that seemed to flow from her head to her toes, like a river running a powerful course right through her body, washing away all tension; she was calm and she stepped surely through the dense brush. Jackie knew that her book, now bound fast to her back, glowed. She knew this, too: that she was heading the right way.

"But who is really free, when others are slaves?" Jackie felt, rather than heard the words. She picked up the pace, still filled with an unnatural calm, given the circumstances.

"Zumbi, Zumbi, here is Zumbi!" This she heard, too, a thrumming that vibrated through the soles of her feet. She surged ahead, carried forward by the beat of the bush.

"Zumbi, Zumbi … Zumbi!" Now she turned her head left and faced him square on; running beside her, stride for stride, was a dark, majestic, smiling man. Zumbi. He was powerfully built, clearly a warrior, but she was not afraid at all.

He pointed and it seemed to Jackie that the very tip of his finger sparked a path where there had been none. He nodded, urging her on. Jackie tried to thank him, but he melted fast into the shadows, and she was alone again one more.

And so she ran. And kept on going. Now the moon shone down on her in full, lighting the way to a destination as yet unknown.

Jon blinked and looked at the document again.

Jackie was gone.

And he sighed, then, as he stepped back into his mother's hospital room. There was nothing he could do for Jackie, and his mother needed him now more than ever. Jackie would just have to handle things on her own. His mother and Petey were still deeply asleep, fingers intertwined, curled into each other despite the tubes that ran from his mother's arms and under her nose. They were bathed in the bluish light of the full moon; despite the late hour, the curtains hadn't yet been drawn.

A nurse stopped by the room, clipboard in hand. She patted Jon on the back, and then quietly set to work, taking careful note of her patient's pulse and heartbeat, ever so careful not to disturb the sleeping woman. When she was done, the nurse looked down at Petey, and her eyes softened.

"I'll let him rest, for now, but when I come 'round in another few hours, let's try to get your brother up, all right, hon?" she said to Jon. "Maybe he can help us with some holiday decorations. Think he'll be up to it?"

"Sure." Jon nodded, confused. He pulled out his cell phone to check the date. November 20. He'd totally forgotten that it was almost Thanksgiving.

"And why don't you take the other one?" She pointed to the unoccupied bed by the door. "I don't believe we'll have any more guests tonight."

Jon thanked her and sat down on the edge of the empty hospital bed. Suddenly he felt terribly tired. He grabbed a pillow and fell into a deep, dreamless sleep. He sank like a stone, his worries floating far, far above him.

Tomorrow's sun is on its way—a relentless sun, inscrutable like life.
—Jose Maria Machado de Assis

Chapter XIII:

Two White Ghosts

BRAZILIAN JUNGLE, 1783

Jackie came to the small clearing and slowed to a walk. Her whole body ached, and her legs were cramping. She shook them out, thankful that she hadn't been running under the glare of the tropical sun. Still, a thin film of sweat covered her entire being, and her shirt was plastered firmly to her back.

The night was warm. Jackie wiped her brow with the back of her linen sleeve. But just as she was bringing her arm down, she saw a sight that made her freeze, her heart beating wildly.

Two figures, so dark that they blended into the night, stepped out of the brush at the edge of the clearing. The men were so similar in manner and bearing they could have been twins. Each carried a tall spear and a shield; each had a dagger bound at his waist. Both wore only white linen pants rolled up at the ankle to expose bare feet.

Jackie's book felt warm against her back, and beneath it, her skin began to tingle.

"Come," said the tall African on the right. "We have been expecting you."

"Thank you," she said, calmed by his manner, and followed the speaker; the other man fell in behind her. She felt perfectly safe and at peace. In the distance, she could make out a clearing surrounded by low huts; a few shadowy figures walked together, murmuring in the night.

Jackie was exactly where she needed to be. She was going home. All at once she was enveloped in a warm, perfumed hug.

"Mom!"

Judith held Jackie out at arms' length for a moment, drinking in the sight of her daughter, who gazed right back at her. She felt, not for the first time, that she was seeing a younger version of herself. Long, curling red hair clung to the napes of their necks, wayward strands having escaped high chignons, twisted up and away from the heat.

At five-six, Judith was still taller than her child, who at fifteen had bemoaned the fact that she was destined to be the "shrimp" of the family. But Jackie was a miniature version of her mother in all other respects. Both were slender; both were fine boned and possessed of porcelain skin; and both had green eyes, only Judith's, interestingly enough, were flecked with gold. And now both were dressed in the costume of the colonial era, except Jackie wore a sailor's clothing, and her mother a washerwoman's garb.

By now a small crowd had gathered around the two Tempos, in spite of the late hour. Small children clung to their mothers' skirts, fearful of the two very strange white women who held hands tightly and laughed out loud in the dark. More people emerged from their sleeping huts, rubbing their eyes at the late hour. Beatriz stood a bit apart, observing the commotion with preternatural calm.

"Isn't this exciting?" Her friend Pedro ran up to her, tugging on her arm. "Now we have *two* white ghosts! I wonder what will happen!"

Beatriz looked at the two pale women. The older one caressed her daughter's hair and hugged her tight. The younger one started to cry. Beatriz was a bit put off by how ugly she turned; her eyes became red and swollen, and her face had red blotches. Not for the first time, she wondered at the strangeness of white people. She shivered, more than a bit repelled.

She spoke softly to her friend. "There is sure to be trouble now. Too many whites in our home."

"But ... but there are only two of them—and they're women!"

"Exactly." Beatriz turned away, leaving Pedro to scratch his head in puzzlement.

He shrugged and turned back to the excitement. "Weird girl."

At that moment, the crowd made way for a woman who, like Beatriz, had been watching Jackie and her mother with some interest. Elva stepped forward to touch Jackie's head. The old woman put her fingers over the teen's face and called out in a guttural voice. Though Jackie flinched, she instinctively trusted the medicine woman.

Then Jackie felt as though she were falling back in time, back to her childhood and even before. She saw the earth, spinning through the deepest darkness; she saw the birth of stars, shattering through the dark. Then she saw no more. She opened her eyes.

Elva had taken her hand away and was peering deep into Jackie's soul.

"Zumbi showed you the way," she stated.

"Yes," Jackie answered softly, wondering how the old woman knew. "He spoke to me …"

"Ah, you are favored. I'm not surprised. Tell me what he said," Elva pressed.

Jackie took a deep breath. "He asked who was really free when others are slaves."

"Yes, that was Zumbi. It is almost time." Elva turned to Judith. "But first, there is something that you both must show to me." She made her way back to her lonely hut, and the two Tempos followed close behind.

Elva shooed away half the village, which followed the three. Still, many of them hung about her hut, wondering at the strange vision of two red-haired women. Finally she came to the door to silence the small crowd: "There will come a time when your courage and strength will be tested. We have all known that this was bound to happen once in our lifetimes."

She paused and looked at the hushed crowd outside her door. A baby whimpered in its mother's arms and burrowed deep into her neck.

"That time is almost at hand. Go home and prepare for war."

At her words, the crowd dissolved into the night. Only Beatriz remained, nestled against the hut. Elva turned back to her guests, who were seated on a mat on her dirt floor, and coaxed a small fire from her cooking twigs.

"I will brew some *guaraná*," she said, "to revive your energy and strengthen your spirit." She pinched a few dried leaves from one of the gourds on a shelf lining her otherwise sparse hut. "And you will tell me everything."

*We have to stop and be humble enough to understand
that there is something called mystery.*
–Paulo Coelho

Chapter XIV:

Under Attack

As the moon began to climb high above the dense forest, the three women settled into the sultry night. Elva passed out cups of *guaraná*; Beatriz curled up outside the medicine woman's door and promptly went to sleep.

"Leave her." Elva put a thick blanket over the girl. "One day she will be my apprentice and will become an *orixá*, a high priestess, if the gods and *Nossa Senhora*, the Virgin Mary, permit. She will have great power as she has never been a slave. She has never been crippled by another's will."

Neither Jackie nor her mother dared ask about Elva's own experience. "Where we come from," said Jackie, "slavery is considered to be a terrible thing. It is wrong to hold another being captive and to force him to work—or worse. We have read of the horrors of the slave trade, and stories told by people who lived during that time have been written down and shared with so many others." She thought for a moment, then blurted out: "Was Zumbi a slave?"

Elva nodded. "Yes, but not for long. He fought for the freedom of all slaves and defied his uncle, who wanted to turn Palmares over to the Portuguese."

Jackie was shocked. "Why would his uncle want to do that?"

Elva shook her head. "Ganga Zumba was tired of fighting and had been promised his own freedom. Then one November, Zumbi was betrayed and captured ... and beheaded."

Jackie drew a sharp breath, and Elva looked the white girl in the eye. "But his spirit lives on in all of us ... and here, in this *mato*, protecting us from harm."

Then Elva gestured at the books before them. "You did not read of Zumbi in the books you carry." This was a statement. Jackie nodded. "And these books work differently from the others." This was not a question, either.

"Yes." Judith clasped her daughter's hand. "These books can take us home—if we heed the right signals."

"Or if we really want to go," Jackie said sadly. She looked away from her mother, eyes filling up with tears.

"Shh,"—Judith's own throat constricted—"you know we have to find Devon and return him to our time—and that all three books must be sent back to their own time as well." She caressed her daughter's hair. "Then this madness will stop."

She stopped at the obvious: why was Devon here, in eighteenth-century Brazil?

"I've always wondered why he never joined up with, you know, Alexander the Great … or Julius Caesar … or Napoleon …" Jackie picked up on her mother's thoughts. "To really change the course of history with what he knows. What does he want, anyway?"

"I'm not sure *he* knows," Judith said ruefully. "Or else he'd be easier to track down."

Elva listened, squatting on her haunches, and threw some small bones and odd twigs within a circle she had traced on the swept dirt floor. She frowned, and threw them again.

"What do they mean?" Jackie asked.

"War." Elva pointed to the way the bones had piled up. "And a great struggle—here." She gestured at a jagged rock on the edge of the circle. "This struggle will continue beyond our lifetimes. And this"—now she pointed to a pitted piece of wood—"signifies illness. But not here. This is a terrible, deadly disease. Strange," she muttered, "it's not from here at all."

"It's not?" Judith shuddered. She thought of how smallpox had been transmitted from Europe to the Americas, nearly wiping out the native Indian population. But it was said that those who died were the lucky ones.

"No." Elva picked up the pocked wood and brought it closer to her face, examining it more closely. "This is not only from another place, it is from another time altogether. It is a cry for help." She looked directly at Jackie. "You know of this."

The teen felt her arms prickle with goose bumps. The only sick person she knew was back at home, in Arborville —Jon's mother. The last she knew, Mrs. Durrie was in a coma, and Jon was rushing to save her. She remembered the look on his face when he dropped her off at Aunt Isobel's, and her heart tightened. He probably still had the document packet she'd shown him when they both scrambled out of school. It seemed like . . . forever ago. Jackie sighed, wondering where he was—and how his mother was doing.

They'd been told there was no cure, and at this point, the doctors were trying to make her as comfortable as possible while she went through the process of … dying. *Palliative care*, Jon had called it, biting off the words with a bitterness so intense she shivered. There was no way out, the doctors had said, and even as they bombarded her body with additional chemotherapy and other treatments, the cancer had continued to spread. Finally, Jon's mother put an end to all traditional treatment. If she was going to die—soon—she wanted to be lucid to the last, so that she could appreciate her children more fully.

What the doctors hadn't anticipated, however, was the determination of this free spirit, who was willing to try all sorts of alternative treatments, from chiropractic sessions and acupuncture to massages and a healing woman's circle. She followed a strict macrobiotic diet: no processed foods, no refined sugar, no caffeine, no meat or dairy products, and few fruits. She ate vegetables, tofu, seaweed, and brown rice. Lots of brown rice. And everything was organic. For once, Jon was glad to wolf down school lunches. Chili burgers were ambrosia after his mom's homemade miso soup with seaweed.

Still, he didn't complain much. Although the cancer was still there, it had stopped spreading, and the tumor in her liver was actually shrinking. The color returned to her cheeks. Jon's mother went to her doctors only for once-monthly CAT scans during that time, and they were puzzled by her turnaround. She wasn't. "Food shall be my medicine, and medicine shall be my food!" she would quote Hippocrates, the Greek father of medicine. "Aren't you supposed to be familiar with the works of Hippocrates?" she'd ask her doctors when they pressed her to come in for more aggressive treatment. "Didn't you take the Hippocratic oath when you graduated?" She was frustrated that none of her doctors had taken so much as a course in nutrition while in medical school.

"I think my mom's cure is going to kill me!" Jon had gagged one afternoon in Dona Marta's kitchen, reaching for a *misto-quente*, a grilled ham and cheese sandwich. He was happy that she was holding her own against the terrible disease, but that didn't make her food any tastier. 'Regular' food was one of the reasons he liked to linger in Aunt Isobel's kitchen, although Dona Marta made everything from scratch and bought only organic foods as well.

But now Jon's mother had landed in the hospital again—and was in a coma. Some sort of mysterious relapse, perhaps, but no one would know until a few more tests were run.

Elva peered at the signs before her. She closed her eyes, listening for the voice of her ancestors to guide her. She shook her head slightly. This was not a vision from the past; it was a voice from the future, a quiet plea for help. And it was connected directly to Jackie.

"This is an illness beyond our time. From the future." She looked at Jackie. "This person needs your help."

It was Jon! Jackie was sure of it. But what could she do? She explained Jon's situation—his mother's illness, her attempts at a cure, and her recent collapse.

"Tell me the symptoms," Elva commanded. Jackie obeyed. The high priestess listened, then hummed a few bars of an African healing song. She began to pull together a remedy. Jackie could barely understand her as she hummed under her breath. "Some *pau d'arco*, yes and powerful *ipê roxo* …a bit of *catauba*…. Bless this potion, dear Virgin Mary." She wrapped it all in a snug pouch, tied it to a string, and then hung it around Jackie's neck.

"There." Elva sat back on her heels. "You will use it, in your own time. You can be sure of that."

Jackie wasn't sure of anything, anymore. Still she had a question: "Why did you invoke the Virgin Mary, and not your own gods?"

"Ah, but we Africans are caught between the worlds," said Elva. Jackie was confused. "All that we had when we came across the great seas were our beliefs. But my own mother taught me about the Virgin Mary. African and Portuguese ideas mixed together are more powerful than one or another alone. This is what it means to be Brazilian, for there is much beauty, but also much violence in this land of mixed cultures," she said, crossing herself for added protection.

It seemed to Jackie then that Jon was right there; she saw his head in his hands, shoulders slumped. Her heart ached for him, and she closed her eyes. The veil between the two worlds had dimmed. She could almost reach out and touch him.

"Jon," she whispered, "you're not alone. We're going to help her. I promise." Tears started in her eyes as she clenched her fists.

Jon lifted his head. He seemed to be looking right at her, and his mouth opened in surprise.

Then the predawn stillness was shattered.

"War!" someone shouted, and the *quilombo* came to life. People spilled out onto the paths; grown men grabbed any weapon they could find and assembled for instructions in the center court.

"We're under attack!"

A terrible scream tore through the jungle.

The spear of the twilight is coming, son, my son
Quick, dodge it!
—Jivaro war song

CHAPTER XV:

THE DANCE OF WAR

RUNAWAY SLAVE COMMUNITY, BRAZIL, 1783

RUNAWAY SLAVE COMMUNITY, BRAZIL, 1783

The *chefe do mato* strode across the court with a calm determination to speak to his men. They were neatly ordered, spears at side, shields in front, short knives secured to their waists. They were used to drilling as a fighting force at least once a week, and every month, the men—from twelve years and up—would head into the jungle for a few days, running hard to build up endurance.

They had been under attack like this once before, and the *quilombo* had survived. Every member of the community knew that Palmares had held off the Brazilian government for more than a hundred years. But when it was finally brought down by Dutch mercenaries and Brazilian soldiers, not one person was captured. It was as if the *quilombeiros*, those who lived there—runaway slaves, mestizos, and those who had been brought up in the safe haven—had simply melted into the *mato*. No traces of them remained, save the cooking fires that were still smoking, and empty huts, in which lingered the smell of daily life, the smell of the quotidian.

And so this *quilombo*, self-sufficient and self-perpetuating, was a direct descendant of Palmares. There were more like it, too, offshoots of resistance and the refusal to accept slavery. It was here, in the *mato*, that they lived in freedom, but not free from fear. The possibility that they would be discovered one day by the slavers was very real. But this keen awareness—of the threats that encroached on them as the nation of Brazil sprawled out from the coastal regions, unfurling like an octopus reaching down the many rivers, more complex and numerous than anywhere else in the world—this knowledge only served to bind the small group ever tighter.

So it was that every ritual, every drill, every meal, every sunrise and sunset was layered with special meaning—this was for protection, that was for the blessings of the gods and above all else that of Jesus Christ and the Virgin Mary, both of whom had suffered for them here on earth while the Father and Holy Ghost looked on. Every day was a blessing, for tomorrow, the older ones knew, might bring suffering, and this they all had experienced, save for the children and the few others who had been born in the wilderness.

But the men were ready, they were willing, and they were armed, not only with very real spears and daggers but also with the knowledge that every last one of them would fight to the death. Freedom was worth more than their lives; the body could be destroyed, but not the spirit.

Jackie looked on at this formidable display of determination and might, her arm around her mother's small waist. Judith hugged her back. She was impressed, but knew that the Brazilians had firepower, guns that could mow them all down in a matter of minutes.

"One of the scouts has returned. The other has gone to *Deus do Céu*—God in the sky," said the *chefe*. The crowd grew silent, knowing full well that the terrible scream they had heard had come from the mother of the dead man, who had been carried back to the *quilombo* all the way from the edge of the *mato*. It was the custom to protect the bodies for a proper send-off to the next world.

That ritual farewell, however, would have to wait. "We know that they are a half-day's march from here, possibly less, as they are advancing very quickly. There are more than two hundred fifty of them, Brazilian and Dutch, traveling upriver by boat."

The crowd gasped and broke into panicked talk.

"There is more." The *chefe's* quiet voice cooled all chatter. "They say that they have a yellow-haired wizard with them, one who carries a strange, magical book and uses it to make predictions and chart courses. It is a book of maps. And this man is leading them to us, for he would create his own empire, and he would begin to do so here."

"Devon!" Jackie gasped. Though the sun was climbing higher, warming the *mato* with its sultry rays, she felt icy inside.

Judith stepped forward. "I can stop him."

The *chefe do mato* crossed his arms. "Impossible, woman. You may be white, but you are unarmed."

"That's not quite true." Judith revealed her own book of maps.

The *chefe* drew back as if burned, and his men stepped back as well. Judith waited, and Jackie held her breath. What on earth was her mother thinking? Then he leaned in. "You can fight him with this?"

"Yes," Judith said, and smiled. "I have the answers right here." And she opened a page to reveal a glowing red line. "He is marching on us—here. This is where he is right now." She pointed to a close-up map of the jungle. "But we can ambush him"—she pointed— "here." The *chefe*'s eyes widened slightly; he was careful not to show emotion, especially not in front of a white woman.

"Is this so?" he demanded of Elva, who was at her side.

She nodded. "She will go ahead," the medicine woman said quietly. "And I will go with her."

"To arms!" the cry went up again. Now everyone spilled out into the center of the *quilombo*. All able-bodied men age twelve and up stood in neat formation under the command of the *chefe do mato*. Everyone else—all the women, children, and very old men—stood back at the mighty display of force and power.

Jackie gasped as more and more people came out of hiding. The very woods, it seemed, would join this rebel army and fight to keep their way safe. She reached for her mother's hand. The two women exchanged a wordless glance that encompassed everything they were feeling—love, fear, hope. For the sake of her mother, Jackie clamped down on a rising panic and turned to look at the proud and determined African, mulatto, and mestizo men in front of her.

More people than she ever imagined in one place— much less a dense jungle—were crowded into the central clearing. The onlookers formed a ring around the warriors, more than ten deep in some places. Somewhere in the crowd, Elva chanted in a low voice; it was impossible to decipher her ancient words, even with the book as guide. Sweat rolled down Jackie's back. She could barely breathe for the heat.

"Ey!" a young warrior called out.

At first, the drumbeat was so low that to Jackie it seemed like the very earth was rumbling quietly, and then the beat and the sound swelled in strength. She saw an old man to her right pick up an odd-looking instrument, just a few long strings attached to a bowlike structure. He began to pick at the strings, which made a challenging, twangy sound. Then the drum seemed to circle round the strings, and it seemed to Jackie that the two instruments were about to fight, daring and backing off, teasing, prodding, provoking.

Two muscular men stepped forward from the formation and began to circle each other with a slow, rhythmic grace. Like the rest of the men, they wore linen pants rolled up slightly past their ankles. They quietly discarded their weapons and faced each other, man to man.

Jackie held fast to her mother's hand. As one man lunged, the other leaned back, and they taunted each other in a wordless dance of death. One man swung his legs around, and the other ducked underneath the deadly kick, spinning away, now on the ground, pushing off with his elbows and kicking back at his opponent. They circled around in a fighting dance, spinning, kicking, twisting on their feet, arms, and heads. Jackie was stunned by this display of power and grace.

"This is *capoeira*," her mother whispered. "I've seen it before, but only as a demonstration. It's a form of martial arts, a blend of West African and Brazilian traditions, unique to Brazil, but possibly transported from the West African coast. No one knows for sure where it originated, possibly in these *quilombos*. Now we know that it was, in fact, practiced here." She gave Jackie's hand a squeeze.

"Yes, Professor Tempo." Jackie smiled and squeezed back. She was transfixed by the men's grace and dignity, by the sheer power with which they pretended to attack each other, by their control as they narrowly missed each other.

Suddenly the music died, and the men stepped back into formation.

The entire *quilombo* went silent. Then Elva stepped out to address the men. She was dressed entirely in white, from the kerchief around her head to her full lace dress. They kneeled at her presence.

"The spirits of our ancestors, those who are linked to us across an ocean of pain, and also the blessed Virgin Mary are with us on this day of reckoning. You will fight with a power unseen, a power that will course through your very blood." She held a chicken in her right hand, and with the left, slit its throat with a small dagger. Blood dripped to the ground, and Elva's eyes rolled back in her head.

"A sacrifice to those who watch over us, may this be the only blood spilt from our *quilombo*!" Jackie started when she heard the small voice of Beatriz. The young girl was dressed as Elva, head to toe in white. She held a black and red candle in each hand, and she lit them now, placing them gently on the ground, propped up by a small pile of stones. She gently took the dead chicken from Elva's hands, and laid it to rest by the candles, murmuring softly as she did so. Then she made the sign of the cross.

A cry rang out: "We will fight to the death!" This was from a fierce-looking young man of no more than twenty. Jackie recognized him—her companion from the slaving ship! He looked strong and glorious now. He caught Jackie's eyes and grinned.

"For freedom!" came another shout from the formation.

"We are not afraid!" He raised his spear. The crowd approved and cheered the men on.

And then just as quickly as they had stepped into formation, the men melted into the shadows of the jungle. Jackie looked around at the rest of the crowd, which was pulling back as well.

"Now what?" she asked Elva, who took her elbow and was guiding her back to her hut.

"Now we go, too. There is a sacred space of refuge. We will be protected." They had arrived at the doorstep of her hut.

"But—you'll leave all this? Isn't it what you are fighting for?" Jackie wondered as Elva carefully picked through her herbs and took her oracle bones.

"No, white girl." The old African smiled. We are fighting for this." She tapped her breastbone. "Our spirit. Our way of life. Our traditions, old and new."

Judith and Beatriz waited for Elva at the doorway, joined by a small crowd.

"Come." Elva motioned to the group of about thirty. Even the babies were hushed. In the distance, Jackie could hear the sounds of battle. Shots rang out, and the very jungle seemed to shudder. "We must hurry." A wild scream pierced the air. The small group drew together and followed Elva into the heart of the jungle, where it was very dark indeed.

UNIVERSITY HOSPITAL, PRESENT TIME

Though the day dawned bright and clear, a terrible chill swept through the hospital room. Petey stirred and turned over, burrowing deeper into the hospital bed next to his mother's. His shirt was dirty, Jon saw, and his jeans were slightly torn. One graying white sock showed the beginnings of a hole. Jon looked at him and sighed. He was such a good kid. Most eleven-year-olds would complain if they didn't have the right clothing so they could be "cool" with their friends. In light of what was happening to their mother, none of that mattered.

Jon blinked fiercely, willing himself to be strong for his brother; Petey looked up to him, and as annoying as he was at times—like when he'd sneak out of the house on Jon's bicycle, or worse, when he dared to set foot in Jon's room without permission—the kid actually helped him, too. When Jon was down, it seemed Petey could help cheer him up. Like the time he said he'd make dinner, and ended up making the best burgers that Jon had ever scarfed down.

"It's all in the technique," he'd told his older brother. "See, ya gotta steam-broil the burger, it's the best way to keep the juices in …" Jon was amazed, all the more so because his football-loving younger brother had carefully served him first and waited for his reaction. "Well?" Jon grinned widely and kept on eating, famished after a really rough workout of sprints.

Outside their mother's hospital room, the corridors were beginning to fill with activity as shifts ended and began and doctors started making their early-morning rounds. Jon got up and stretched his long legs; he didn't think he'd slept at all the night before. He kept hearing all sorts of strange noises, and when he started to drift off, he imagined Jackie tied to a stake, surrounded by flames and crazy dancing people. He shook his head clear and went over to the window. The parking lot was empty at this early hour, save for his own car and those of a few other unfortunates who had stayed the night. For a moment, he was overcome with fear over Jackie and his mother—and what would happen to him and Petey? *At least it was a Saturday*, he thought ruefully. He didn't have to worry about getting through another day of school, pretending that everything was normal while the other kids talked about stupid stuff.

Jon shut his eyes then, and it seemed to him that he heard a strange thrumming through the hospital floor. He felt wretchedly sick. But he couldn't be sick now. *C'mon, man*, he told himself, *this too shall pass*. This was his mother's favorite saying, and he used it as a mantra to get him through tough races, when his lungs felt like they were on fire and he thought he was going to die. He'd been telling himself this more often lately, like now—when he looked over at his mother, still unconscious, a terrible shade of gray, hooked up to tubes that barely kept her alive.

The door clicked open quietly. It was Dr. Mahmood, a trim woman in her fifties, making her rounds. Jon's mother was her first patient of the day.

"Looks like the Durrie clan had a sleepover," she said, smiling softly. Jon liked her. She talked directly to him as if he were an adult, unlike some of the other patronizing doctors who had the annoying habit of speaking to him as if he were Petey's age. She tucked her shoulder-length, jet-black hair behind her ears and looked him right in the eye. "We're going to have to ask you and Petey to leave now. We're going to run a whole bunch of tests," she said softly.

Jon nodded, and over her shoulder saw waiting nurses and technicians. He was grateful that she spoke to him first and held the staff back so that he could get Petey out of the way on his own. He nodded wordlessly, and shook his younger brother awake. The two of them kissed their mother good-bye and made their way out of the room. They passed through the maze of bright, sterile hospital corridors and picked their way carefully across the icy parking lot to Jon's car.

Dr. Mahmood stood by the hospital window and watched the two boys drive away. Long schooled against giving in to her emotions, she turned to the staff waiting for her instructions.

"Okay, we're going to run another complete set of tests," she told them. "Let's see if we can't find some answers." She just had to try one more time.

But the woman on the bed was further from death than anyone could imagine.

A stranger has big eyes but sees nothing.
—African proverb

CHAPTER XVI:

SPIDERS AND SPIRITS

BRAZILIAN JUNGLE, 1783

"Time is running out!"

Devon urged his men on. They were a motley group of *bandeirantes* —adventurers, mercenaries, and soldiers—as well as anyone else who was interested and hungry enough to venture into the Brazilian interior to hunt down the *quilombeiros*, the runaway slaves who had set up their own free community in the jungles of Brazil. *Bandeirantes* were known for their lust for adventure; Jorge himself had once been a *bandeirante*, until a more profitable—and for him, enjoyable—opportunity came along as overseer for old Mr. da Silva. Hacking through the *mato*, however, he felt a twinge of regret—how he missed the excitement of the chase, and the pillage and plunder that was so often his reward. His bloodlust had not diminished over time.

Jorge aside, most of Devon's crew knew that tracking and destroying a *quilombo* was a near impossible task. It had taken nearly a century for the Brazilian government to destroy Palmares—the betrayal and beheading of Zumbi finished the *quilombo* once and for all. Yet everyone knew that there were survivors, and the *matos* of Pernambuco were deep enough to hold the continuing trickle of runaways.

Still, the rewards Devon offered were rich enough. Free land, and some slaves to boot.

This hunt was Devon's revenge on the runaway Africans. How dare they abandon him as king? With all his knowledge, and all his power?

He fumed as he thought of how the Africans had disappeared in the torrential downpour, Judith Tempo with them. Flushed with shame, he hacked his way through the steaming jungle with renewed fervor. He recalled how the book remained silent after the downpour and his abandonment, but he had been able to pick his way back to town and find Jorge, the overseer of the da Silva plantation. It was Jorge who had told him of the runaways, Jorge who longed to destroy all *quilombos* once and for all, and the thought pleased him; now *that* would send a message to all those who dared to hope for freedom. Devon offered to set up the entire enterprise.

Now the word had gotten out around town, and plantation owners and government officials were abuzz with excitement. *Quilombos* were a double threat, thanks to the legacy of Zumbi: not only did they offer a safe haven for runaways, but their men would regularly raid the plantations for tools and crops, and to free slaves.

Every able-bodied man who had the courage to join Devon and Jorge tagged along.

So now here they were, several hundred men strong, armed to the teeth with muskets and sabres. From memory, Devon pointed out the signs to the *quilombo*. But after two days in the jungle, the men were growing restless.

"How do we know we're going the right way?" one of the soldiers growled, miserable in his armor. He was distrustful of the *mato* and felt as if he were being watched every minute.

"I know the way, trust me. Why else would I be in this godforsaken place?" Devon snapped. He was wet with perspiration. He pointed to an odd carving in the tree trunk. "See that! We're drawing near!"

Indeed, they had just stumbled upon an outpost of the *quilombo*; it was clear that this was a security point, with a well-camouflaged hut and small fire pit. Jorge found one of the guards and quickly slit his throat. The other melted into the jungle shadow, and his pursuers shot after him to no avail.

"Now that was stupid!" Devon was growing tired of this sadistic man. "We could have used him to find out about the *quilombo*! Idiot!"

Jorge looked down at his blood-covered hands; it was true that he had acted too quickly. The killing had been clean. Better that he should have tortured the runaway, extracted a confession, and then … He was aware that his temper was getting out of hand, and he cut himself as a reminder.

Devon turned away, disgusted. At this rate, they were going nowhere—fast. He wished his book, which was sticking to his chest in the high humidity of the jungle, would show him a way out. This whole adventure was getting way too annoying, and he wanted to go home. He shook his head. Home was not an option. Still, he'd much rather be anywhere else, maybe floating high above it all on a Persian rug like in the story of Aladdin, a gorgeous, bejeweled girl by his side—

"Halt!" A ghastly shriek shattered his reverie and brought him back to earth, groaning at the discomfort of it all. Now what? Could things go any more wrong?

Not a hundred feet ahead, the oldest woman he had ever seen seemed to float above the earth, arms outstretched, moaning. Her face was smooth, but her eyes held a terrible knowledge of the ages; her long, wild white hair flamed around her head like a protective halo. Devon's men froze, then most dropped to their knees.

"*É um espírito,*" one of the soldiers whispered fearfully, "a spirit!" Even Jorge seemed wary. He made the sign of the cross.

"Oh, for God's sake!" Devon stomped his foot. "She's just an old lady, can't you see?" But his men ignored him and whimpered as she raised her arms. He stood his ground. "Look, she's probably standing on some sort of ledge, or tree stump, or something. Let's go!" He would not be intimidated by this ancient being.

Elva was dressed head-to-toe in white, her face marked by ashes, her hair loose and straggling down to her waist. She pointed right at Devon, and he staggered back under the intensity of her glare.

"Oh, you are a sick, sick man. I could curse you, but already you are doomed to wander the earth from past to present, crossing against the currents of time in search of that which you will never possess." Her eyes widened, and from one hundred feet away, he could see that her irises were blue. He was shocked—did she know about the book?

"You will leave this place now, this time, and return to wander through the darkness, through night and day, across time and space," Elva intoned. "Go now and mingle with the living—and the dead! This is the curse you yourself have wrought and are destined to endure until you repent and see the error of your ways! Go!"

Devon's men moaned, crouching in the underbrush that they might escape the wrath of Elva. Even Jorge sank down, pale beneath his sun-reddened skin. Then he gave a great shout and backed into one of the *bandeirantes*.

"*Olha aqui*! Look here!" He pointed at the ground, which seemed to be moving beneath his feet. Then it surged over his boots.

One of the *bandeirantes* leapt back in terror. "*Aranhas!*" He crashed through the brush as the wave of big black spiders sped after him. Jorge swiped them furiously off his arms, and then all the men took off, scattering throughout the dense jungle as fast as they could.

Devon shook with fear as the tide swarmed toward him. "Get me out!" he shouted, furious at being abandoned once more. A spider skittered up his leg, moving faster than he could react.

Then Devon's book began to warm, and quickly became uncomfortably hot. In spite of his fear, he reached inside his shirt—it was burning now, and he felt as if he were being branded on the spot—and ripped it out, heedless of the shocked men nearby. He flipped through the pages, and it seemed to him that his whole body was on fire, from his toes to the very ends of his hair.

"Go, go, and never return to this place. I forbid it ..." Elva's voice rang in his ears, and continued to thrum through his entire being long after she ceased to speak. His eyes felt like they were melting in their sockets, and he rifled through the book in desperation, seeing nothing. Jorge was long gone now, tearing quickly through the jungle, frantic to get out of these evil woods.

And then in a blinding flash, Devon was gone, too.

Is it both mine and yours this
destiny that binds us (together)
no matter how much it is denied
—Fado

CHAPTER XVII:

HOMEWARD BOUND

Elva had led them through the darkest part of the *mato,* sure of foot, as if the ancients were showing her the way. Jackie could not fathom how Elva knew where to go, as they twisted and turned through what seemed to be impenetrable undergrowth.

But the going was easy—easier, it seemed, than it should have been as they hastened to follow the medicine woman. As if on cue, the *mato* opened before her and the group marched single file; even the children were quiet. Judith reached back to touch Jackie once in a while as they marched in semidarkness to the place where Elva said they'd be safe.

Jackie first felt, rather than heard, a deep rumbling that seemed to come from the very center of the earth. As they followed Elva, the vibrations became noise, and then the pounding seemed to reverberate throughout her entire being. Still, she was not afraid. Tight across her chest, inside her shirt, her book was warm, a sign that she had come to recognize meant they were heading the right way.

"There." Elva led them to the edge of a clearing and pointed down. They stared into a chasm. A huge waterfall dropped several hundred feet and pounded the rocks below. "Follow me." She began to pick her way down, nimble as a ten-year-old. Beatriz followed closely. Jackie hung back, unsure, as the others filed past her, winding down, down it seemed to the earth's very core. She could barely make out the bottom for the spray. The crash of water roared in her ears.

"Pumpkin." Her mother used her special term of endearment for her daughter. Her damp red hair mirrored Jackie's, curling 'round her ears. "It's time to go." The last woman had begun the descent, a baby tied fast to her back. Jackie sighed, and nodded. She was so tired of all this craziness; all she wanted was to be home with her parents, in *normal* time, curled up with a good book and drifting off to sleep on the couch. But there was no way to go but forward. Or, in this case, down.

There was no way to tell how long they had couched in the grotto behind the thick curtain of water that plummeted past them to the bottom of the chasm. While it was damp there, it was warm, too, though not quite as hot as the outside. They were so close to the water—indeed it was all around them—but they were safe, unseen to the outside world. All anyone who peered down would see was a cascade of water pounding mercilessly on the rocks below. And there were nearly three dozen women and children behind that barrier.

The children played quietly, and Jackie nestled against her mother, soaking in her warmth and love. If only they could hold on to this moment. If only her father were here—or better yet, if only they were all back home and this was one long, agonizing dream. But she was safe now. They all were. Elva had slipped away for now, but a feeling of peace and calm had filtered through the group when she gave them a blessing to protect against evil spirits and men. She would give a sign when it was safe to return; Beatriz was entrusted as lookout.

Jackie slipped beneath a first hazy layer of slumber, mindful of the world around her but unable to respond. Then quickly, she was deeply asleep, sinking fast into forgetfulness and dark, losing herself and glad of it, cushioned by everything and nothing at once.

Down she sank, and out of the void of the deepest sleep, images, unbidden, unfurled and reached for her.

First she saw Devon, dressed in flowing silk robes, his face contorted with frustration and rage, clutching his book, running through a fantastical city of towers and spires, up the stairs of a large building decorated with arabesque patterns—and then disappearing into the dark.

Then she heard her aunt Isobel's voice. "Remember … follow the Middle Road home. Look for the door …." Jackie stirred, and a vague recollection of previous travels in ancient China tickled the edges of her consciousness. She would not be long in this world, then.

She saw her father, determined, tracking them down in this very jungle. He knew that Devon had moved on, and he and Judith needed to pursue him into the next world, wherever that was.

And then she saw Jon, his arm around Petey, as they walked up to the hospital to visit their mother. She could see that he was struggling to be brave. He bit his lip, and in her sleep, Jackie bit hers, too.

A warm hand pressed on her shoulder, and Jackie slowly awoke, the pounding of the waterfall making its way into her consciousness. The grotto was empty save for Judith and Beatriz. Jackie sat up slowly.

"You have visited the world of the *orixá*, the land of spirits, and have been given a great gift," the young girl told Jackie, her eyes clouding over with an unseen vision.

Jackie smiled ruefully at the girl as Judith looked on, not without a hint of sadness. "How so?" Jackie asked Beatriz. "Some strange dreams, sure, but—"

"Shh." Beatriz put a finger to Jackie's lips. "What did your dreams tell you?"

"Beatriz!" It was Pedro now, calling his friend on. "Hurry up! We're almost at the top and we're going home!"

Jackie sat up straighter then, and both Judith and Beatriz explained quickly how the battle was over almost before it had started. How Elva had clambered up over an ancient temple, now overgrown with vines, and invoked the ancient gods of their ancestors to protect them. How the attacking soldiers and mercenaries fled in fear, the full *quilombo* fighting force in hot pursuit, mindful of the weapons the white men carried but determined to chase them out of their world. For they would protect their freedom, and that of their children, with their lives, if necessary, and wanted to send a message to all the slavers and those who abetted their inhuman and immoral practice.

"But we will move again tomorrow, so now we make haste to prepare," Beatriz added.

"For what?" Jackie's head was pounding.

Beatriz smiled deeply. "To go deeper into the *mato*— deep into the interior."

"Why are you smiling, then?" Jackie asked. "You're leaving your home, the only one you've known all your life."

Beatriz shook her head.

"No, my home is inside me; I will carry the spirits of our ancestors from across the wide ocean with me wherever I go. This is home," she said, and she pressed a small hand to her chest. "Here, too." She tapped her dark head. "This body is my home, even if I am taken from my people one day. But that will not happen." She smiled, noting the look of alarm on the two white women's faces. "My vision has been realized; I see no other threats to our group."

"Beatriz, hurry *up*!" Now Pedro was insistent, and slapped his fist against his thigh.

Beatriz stood up, and held a small hand out to Jackie. "You have your own path, as does your mother. You have separate but shared destinies." She looked hard at Judith and Jackie. "You have missions to fulfill. I can tell you that you will be together again someday—indeed, your family will be made whole again."

"When?" Jackie was torn at the thought of leaving her mother. Her book was warm, and she pulled it out.

"In time," Beatriz responded evenly, and walked out of the grotto, disappearing up the steep path by whence they had descended.

Jackie held her mother tight; it seemed impossible that they could ever be separated again.

"Where's Dad?" Judith pulled out her own book, and showed Jackie the map. "Here." She pointed to a glowing red line that led deep into the Brazilian interior.

"But ... he doesn't have the book—you do!" Jackie said.

Her mother smiled. "I know; that's why we're going to go get him." She pulled her daughter out from behind the thundering falls. "Just before we left the *quilombo*, Elva told me that she had sent for him, using her secret guides. Your father has made it here, and he's waiting for us at the top." She started slowly up the steep path. She turned back to her daughter. "Maybe he was guided, too, by the ghost of Zumbi?"

Jackie's heart pounded at the thought of seeing her father. It was all too weird. She struggled behind her mother, careful not to lose her footing on the switchbacks. She grabbed at the brush and roots for balance.

Judith disappeared over the top.

"Wait!" Jackie called out, and her mother's face reappeared—joined by a very scraggly version of her father! Jackie looked up, dizzy, and noted the trees arching into the night sky, lit up by a million bright stars, framing their loving faces. *Like a door*, Jackie thought. The book glowed against her chest, but she didn't need it to see where she was headed. She was going home. David Tempo grinned down at his daughter and held out his hand, and Jackie reached for it with joy, this one last step …

And she would have cried, if she could, if she hadn't crossed the threshold, if she weren't caught between two worlds, scarcely able to breathe for being pulled forward in time, whirling and slamming through space. She saw her father, distraught, staring wildly into the night, scanning the sky in desperation; her mother buried her face in her hands. Then they turned away from the edge of the gorge and went back into the jungle. Seeing without seeing, she knew that Elva was leading her people deeper into the jungle, her young apprentice by her side. She saw a man who had once evoked terrible fear among the slaves lead them to the edge of the *mato*—"Go! Run!" His soul was heavy with past misdeeds; surely he could start to make amends, and the freed slaves backed away into the *mato* with little more than the shirts on their backs, made mute by

Jorge's strange actions, and they began to run, searching for their land of freedom.

Jackie saw all this, and she knew it to be true, and she gave herself over to the rush of time and space and colliding worlds because there was nothing else for her to do, not now, at least.

When you want something, all the universe conspires in helping you to achieve it.
—Paulo Coelho

CHAPTER XVIII:

H⊕PE

AUNT ISOBEL'S MANSION, PRESENT TIME

"Figures. Thought you'd be here by now." The deep voice sounded familiar, and then a wet nosed nudged Jackie. She turned her face away, deep into her aunt's Persian carpet.

Jackie's dog was persistent. "Cut it out, Wolfe!" She pushed him away by reflex, and she was suddenly aware of her surroundings. She sat up, a little shaky, and reached for him. "Sorry, boy. I've missed you so much." She buried her face deep in his shaggy neck, mildly conscious of the fact that Jon was crouching next to her.

"Are you talking to me or the dog?" Jon asked in an amused voice. But when Jackie looked up, she noted a deep sadness etched in his face; his dark blue eyes held an unspoken grief, and his hair was more disheveled than usual. She reached for him and gave him a hug.

"I'm so sorry," she whispered.

"Oh, she's not gone—yet," Jon answered grimly. "But I have to get back soon. Petey's doing homework by her bedside, and I don't think he can hold it together much longer."

"I want to see her," Jackie said softly. Her own mother was traveling to another world, far beyond her reach, but Jon's situation was worse. He could lose his mother forever. "I think I have something that might help." She patted the small pouch of herbs from Elva that dangled from her neck. "It might be worth a try."

"Fine, then." Jon didn't question what it was. The doctors had given up on his mother; he knew that they were just waiting until … she died. He blinked back tears of despair and pulled Jackie to her feet. "And— thanks. I could use the company."

They walked out of Aunt Isobel's mansion to where Christine, Jon's beat-up car, awaited them. The day was clear, bright, and cold, a far cry from the jungles of Brazil. Jackie gave a quick shiver and hugged herself as she stepped into Jon's car.

She grinned at the well-worn seats, and punched some foam padding back into place. "God, I forgot how ugly this car was."

Jon gave a short laugh; it was good to see him crack a smile. "Excuse me. I forgot you're used to traveling in, um, style."

"Certainly a lot faster than this rusty old thing," she countered.

"Faster than the speed of light?" He backed out of the gravel driveway.

"Yeah—more than you know," Jackie answered. She patted her aunt's book.

"Oh, I know all right, thank you very much," he laughed and the two of them bantered all the way back to University Hospital, staying the terrible fear that Jon's mother was slipping away with every second that passed.

Everything comes to an end, reader.
—José Maria Machado de Assis

CHAPTER XIX:

TRUTH AND HEALING

It didn't take long for Elva's herbs to take effect. She had instructed that they should be ground into a fine paste and mixed with a spoon of honey and warm water "to stimulate the senses," she had explained to Jackie, who had no trouble procuring a disposable packet of honey from the hospital cafeteria.

"For my tea," she explained cheerfully to a disinterested serving woman, who did not notice that Jackie was holding a cup of hot water instead. She had waved the redhead on.

Back in the hospital room, Jackie prepared the potion. Petey had fallen asleep again, his mouth open, homework and math book on the floor. This was just as well, for how could she and Jon explain that they were going to spoon the strange-smelling stuff into his comatose mother's mouth?

She concentrated on the task. Elva had told her that her clarity of intent was just as important as the ingredients themselves. "Clear your mind of doubt;

open your soul to truth and healing." Jackie closed her eyes and took a deep breath; she felt herself settle. She seemed to soar high above a beautiful white coast and then down, down, deep into a rich jungle; and then she heard the words *Who is really free?* and she was ordered to let go … just let go, and she did. She opened her eyes; as Jon held up his mother's head, it seemed that once again Jackie could actually see between two worlds, and that Elva was right beside her, chanting softly and nodding in approval. "Good work, *minha filha*—my child."

Jon drew a sharp breath, and Jackie came to focus on his mother, whose eyes were fluttering. He leaned in. "Mom?" His voice was hoarse with emotion, and at that, Petey sat straight up, knocking the rest of his homework on the chair.

It seemed as if the whole world stood still as the boys' mother slowly opened her eyes. She reached out and touched both her sons' cheeks. "Hey guys," she said, smiling weakly, and Jackie quietly slipped out of the room to make her way back home.

"You didn't have to leave," Jon told her later, when they were in Aunt Isobel's grand library.

Jackie clambered down the book ladder and threw herself into her favorite plush velvet wing chair. She had just set the ancient book high on the bookshelf, next to the *Travels of Ibn Battuta*. "Seems like a good spot for it, don't you think?" she asked with a rueful smile.

Once he could see that his mother seemed better, Jon had returned to Shangri-La to thank Jackie. "The doctors are completely stunned—they've run all sorts of tests to find out why she woke up with a hearty appetite, and they discovered that her cancer is completely gone. They actually tried to get Mom to sign herself over for medical research—on sudden remission in cancer patients—but she's sick of hospitals and all that stuff. She just wants to go home."

"I don't blame her," Jackie had agreed. Then he stayed for dinner; Petey was at a friend's house. After Dona Marta nodded approvingly at the cleared plates— *finalement!*—they retired to the library, where Jon asked Jackie about her own parents.

She told him everything as best as she was able, starting with the experience of traveling aboard a slaving ship. He was appalled.

"I knew it was bad, but …" His voice trailed off, and Jackie continued with her story, deep into the night, until she stumbled over describing her last glimpse of her parents.

Jon patted her back awkwardly. "By the way, I knew you'd be okay," he said. "You're good at handling, uh, a challenge."

"Thanks a lot," she snapped. "I'm glad one of us had confidence in my future." She was annoyed. Why did everyone—Aunt Isobel, Jon, her parents—always assume that she could take care of herself? *It wasn't fair*, she thought, miffed. It would be nice to be taken care of for once, instead of always having to be so … tough.

Jon smiled and pulled a wadded-up document packet out from his back pocket. "Check it out. Look at document five."

She took the paper from him and gasped. Gone was the bound woman—Jackie's mother—being taunted by a man behind a frightening African mask. In its place was an engraving of an African dance, and a description of how the slaves held fast to their traditions in the New World.

"Now check out 5b." Jon pointed to the spot.

Jackie scanned the document and smiled. It was another image of a traditional high priestess, and a description of how she incorporated West African and Christian traditions. She took a closer look. It was Elva, and little Beatriz was by her side. The caption noted that the *orixá*, or high priestess, was thought to be able to travel between the world of the living and the world of the dead; she could see the past and well into the future, and was reported to have traveled with red-haired spirits as guides, assisting them in their journeys as well.

Jackie leaned back, then, and looked up at Jon. "I just wish I knew how this is all going to end up," she said, thinking of her mother, her father, and Devon. "I guess I just have to have faith that it'll all turn out okay." She hugged a velour pillow and looked down at the floor.

Jon reached for her hand. "It will," he said, and before he could say another word, Dona Marta shooed him out.

"*Para fora*, young man. Get out! It's well past midnight, and time to go to sleep!" He knew better than to argue with the stubborn Brazilian housekeeper, and promised to come around the next day with more news. He started up his rattling car and drove off into the clear night.

But Jackie was on edge, long after she had sipped the last of her chamomile tea and tucked into bed wearing her favorite old flannel pajamas, Wolfe curled up and snoring at her feet. She tossed and turned as the bright moonlight streamed into her room. It was two in the morning.

"I give up," she announced to the sleeping dog, and wandered through the dark into her aunt's library. It was so bright outside that she didn't need to switch on the lights as she went. Once inside the library, however, she turned on a small Tiffany table lamp.

"Hmm …" She was getting cold now, and wrapped one arm around herself as she traced the worn spines with her free hand. "Hmm …" A medieval mystery; sounded interesting. She pulled out the book and in her haste dropped it to the floor.

As she bent to retrieve it, it seemed to her that the swirling patterns of the Persian carpet rose up to meet her, climbing up her legs and holding her fast, and she stumbled a bit, overwhelmed by the rich colors and repeating designs.

Jackie shook her head and hugged the unread book to her chest. "Wolfe!" she called. The old dog came trotting in right away. Jackie sank into a nearby sofa, grateful for its plush velvet warmth. "C'mon up!" She patted the space beside her, and Wolfe was there in a flash. He turned around once, then put his head in her lap and was instantly asleep. She stroked his head, grateful for his constant companionship. *When I'm living in this world, that is*, she thought ruefully.

Tucking a stray curl behind her ears, Jackie opened her new book. Wolfe stiffened and growled in his sleep; something hovered just beyond Jackie's peripheral vision. She scanned the room quickly—nothing. Outside, as frigid air rattled the windowpanes, Jackie knew that the Atlantic Ocean pounded the base of the cliff without letup, and that the trees surrounding Shangri-La had no choice but to bow to the will of the fierce New England wind.

Jackie was restless; *it's going to be a long night*, she thought. She settled in to read, losing herself in another time and place where her worries had no meaning. She gripped the book as the story began to unfold, vaguely aware that it was here that she was in full control of events; it was here that she was finally safe.

THE END

Author's Note

Jackie Tempo and the Ghost of Zumbi is a work of historical fiction. As such, it is rooted in fact, embellished for the purpose of storytelling.

The 16th century marked the advent of truly global trade, and this included humans who were forcibly transported across the Atlantic from Western Africa to the Americas. How did they retain any sense of their humanity, uprooted as they were from family, tradition, and ancestral lands?

One form of resistance to such European oppression in the Americas was the retention of traditional beliefs. Thus evolved the syncretic nature of Latin American culture, for example, and in particular where African, Indian and European beliefs merged to become known as "Brazilian".

A more overt form of rebellion – in large part due to geography in the Caribbean and in Brazil - was the creation of runaway slave communities, many of which were inaccessible to official powers well into the 20th century. In 17th century Brazil, Palmares was one such *quilombo,* a safe haven for runaway Africans, Indians and meztisos. Its most famous leader was the great Zumbi, who was born in freedom on the *quilombo,* captured and enslaved as a child, and who made his way back to defend this refuge.

In Brazil, Zumbi of Palmares is a hero to many. November 20 is celebrated as the day of National Black Consciousness; this date marks the anniversary of his death in 1695.